Nicholas Shakespeare v
and grew up in the Fai
is the author of *The V*
of the Somerset Maugh... ...u Betty Trask Awards;
The High Flyer, for which he was nominated as one
of Granta's Best of Young British Novelists; *The
Dancer Upstairs*, and most recently, *Inheritance*. His
non-fiction includes *In Tasmania*, winner of the 2007
Tasmania Book Prize, and an acclaimed biography of
Bruce Chatwin. He is a Fellow of the Royal College of
Literature.

Also by

Fiction
The Vision of Elena Silves
The High Flyer
The Dancer Upstairs
Snowleg
Secrets of the Sea
Inheritance

Non-fiction
Bruce Chatwin
In Tasmania
Priscilla: the Hidden Life of an Englishwoman in
Wartime France

Nicholas Shakespeare

ODDFELLOWS

VINTAGE BOOKS
Australia

A Vintage book
Published by Random House Australia Pty Ltd
Level 3, 100 Pacific Highway, North Sydney NSW 2060
www.randomhouse.com.au

First published by Vintage in 2015

Addresses for companies within the Random House Group can be found at
www.randomhouse.com.au/offices

National Library of Australia
Cataloguing-in-Publication entry (paperback)

Shakespeare, Nicholas, author.
Oddfellows/Nicholas Shakespeare.

ISBN 9780857987181 (paperback)

World War, 1914–1918–Australia–Fiction.
Australian fiction.
Broken Hill (N.S.W.)–Fiction.

823.914

Cover design by Christabella Designs
Cover photograph © Pinkcandy/Shutterstock
Typeset in 11/17 pt Sabon by Post Pre-press Group, Brisbane
Printed in Australia by Griffin Press, an accredited ISO AS/NZS 14001:2004
Environmental Management System printer

Random House Australia uses papers that are natural, renewable and recyclable
products and made from wood grown in sustainable forests. The logging
and manufacturing processes are expected to conform to the environmental
regulations of the country of origin.

To M. B.

One

It's a little before 10 am on New Year's Day 1915, and the sun strikes broadside the picnickers waiting at Sulphide Street station. Hats and parasols give faint protection to the 1239 men, women and children who sit or stand in the open ore-wagons, clutching spiky handles of wicker hampers, mopping temples, pointing.

The thermometer registers 101 in the shade.

Since August, many of the same faces have been seeing off volunteers to join the Commonwealth Expeditionary Forces. Now it's their turn to board a train from this station, with 'Broken Hill' painted in black on a white board.

Dressed in freshly laundered summer clothes, the last passengers hurry along the platform and clamber into the trucks which the Silverton Tramway Company has hosed out for them.

Four trucks away from the locomotive that is being stoked up, Mrs Rasp, a podgy, flat-faced woman whose masculine features remind some of the Prime Minister, tells Mrs Kneeshaw in a breathless voice about the letter she has received from her son Reginald.

His infantry squad has arrived in Egypt!

'He says the canal is only 100 yards wide . . . and there's hardly a tree for miles. You'd think you were outside Broken Hill . . .' She wipes a trickle of sweat from the bridge of her big nose, and resumes, fanning her face. '. . . They are near the place where the Children of Israel were supposed to have crossed the Red Sea.' Her straw hat shimmers at the news; she has bought it for the picnic outing at her favourite drapery store in Argent Street.

Mrs Rasp is floury-white, large and shapeless, like her thoughts, and the shapeless things she says. A captain of the League of the Helping Hand, she has that inattention to the opinions of others that one often associates with a double-barrelled name. Her round head cranes forward beneath its halo of cream straw. 'He wants me to send him a balaclava sleeping cap, as he's likely to be exposed to severe cold during the European winter.' She is anxious not to lose Mrs Kneeshaw's attention.

Seated quietly opposite in a rose silk dress, Mrs

Kneeshaw shields her screwed-up eyes with a flattened hand and says nothing.

Since September, Winifred Kneeshaw has managed the Red Cross Society tea-room in Argent Street. She is an elegant woman who has completed her training with the local Red Cross Society and gained her certificate for proficiency in ambulance work – afterwards, she will say that she didn't expect to be called upon so soon to use her knowledge. She finds it hard in this heat to focus on Reginald Rasp in Egypt.

This is a day to forget absent ones. To set aside unwelcome thoughts of war. In a moment, the whistle will shriek, and the train will steam out of the station, ferrying its cheerful cargo not to Adelaide, and from there across the Indian Ocean to Suez – but fourteen miles north-west, along the narrow gauge line to Silverton.

New Year's Day is Manchester Unity Day, and the friendly society's picnic, organised by the Manchester Unity Independent Order of Oddfellows, the greatest gathering of the year in Broken Hill. Today is for those left behind, so far as Mrs Kneeshaw behind her screening fingers is concerned. An opportunity for everyone to draw together and to show their sense of communality after one of the most testing periods in the town's history.

For sixteen years, the metals mined from Broken Hill have been railroaded to Port Pirie and shipped to the Saxon city of Freiberg, 'the Mecca of ores', to make bullets for the Kaiser's guns. But Australia is at war with Germany. For the fifth successive month, the conical heaps of zinc and lead concentrates have piled up untouched. Abandoned, like the German Club in Delamore Street.

'I just wish we could borrow some of Reggie's cool weather,' Mrs Kneeshaw murmurs, and pulls up the corner of her dress and wipes her eye, revealing to Mr Dowter, sitting straight as in a pew beside Mrs Rasp, a flash of white petticoat.

Not wishing to draw attention by too immediately averting his gaze, Clarence Dowter goes on staring with pursed lips and a wooden expression in the direction of Mrs Kneeshaw's exposed underclothes. He is the town's Sanitary Inspector, and has agreed to officiate this afternoon as umpire in the women's seventy-five-yard race at the picnic ground. He is a short, mournful-looking Irishman with a downturned mouth, a forehead dented like his homburg hat, a mop of blue-black hair that competes oddly with his sparse, much fairer beard, and small grey eyes that miss nothing. In the raging sun, his hollowed-out face seems on the verge of melting. Head cocked at an angle, he taps his cigarette on a silver case, and, after an interval which he decides is long enough, shifts his glance to Mrs Lakovsky's latest baby.

'Don't go tiring yourself, mate!'

Mrs Rasp twists with her mouth open to see who it is that Roy Sleath, the policeman's son, is trying to grab the attention of.

It's not hard to recognise the young man who leaps agilely aboard, clasping a bulging brown paper bag: he is of the more athletic type of Broken Hill miner, all elbows, with sandy hair and sharp nose.

'Hey, Ollie, over here!'

Waving down Roy's incitements, he stops in front of Lizzie Filwell, a pale fourteen-year-old with dark brown hair and a prematurely corrugated forehead, and opens her hand. To the girl's obvious delight, he drops a yellow peach into it. He chats with her parents, sitting on either side of her, glances quickly around, and vanishes from view, then reappears, erect, in front of Roy, and chucks him under the chin, before moving on.

For Lizzie's elder sister Rosalind, seated in the same wagon, the day promises something momentous.

Rosalind Filwell wears a white skirt to her ankles, which, like her hands and feet, she wants to be more dainty than they are, and a pomegranate-pink felt hat fringed with a muslin veil to fend off the sun and the flies. Her abundant black hair is tied into a French knot above her oval face. Her deep-set hazel eyes cast their own shadow, so that according to the angle of her face she can seem attractive or plain. When they fix on Oliver Goodmore, the man pushing his way towards her, she looks tired.

One month shy of her twenty-second birthday, Rosalind is certain that Oliver intends to use the pretext of the afternoon's events – the picnics under the pepper trees, the distribution of dolls and lollies, the running events (where he is expected to shine) – to escort her at some point along the dried creek-bed, there being no strong breeze or dust, and propose.

She knows this because her best friend, Mary Brodribb, who waved to her just now from the adjacent truck, personally helped Oliver to select the engagement ring in Harvey's jewellery store.

But is this what Rosalind wants?

She looks up at him in his low-neck flannel shirt and narrow-brimmed hat, with the sun striking his unprotected chin, and his squinting face smiles down at her. His ticket says second class, but from everything in his manner he feels in first.

He throws a leg over the wooden plank which Mrs Rasp has earlier dusted with her fan, and holds out his paper bag. 'Hey, Ros, put these in your hamper, will you, because I'll probably drop them, knowing me.'

Her hands occupied in packing away his peaches and apples, he reaches out to touch Rosalind's cheek with a thick index finger, which has a crescent of dirt she cannot avoid observing.

'Did you sort out Tom's motorbike?'

He doesn't answer her, still puzzled by something.

'I was looking for you over there,' and squeezes in beside her on the temporary wooden bench. 'I reckoned you'd be with Lizzie.'

Two

Rosalind had risen early, woken by a dog. She lay in bed and listened to the howl rising and falling. A harmless noise by day, the cry swept through her like the phantom of her brother's voice, and in the small hot bedroom whipped her thoughts into a mob of skittish anxieties that gathered her off on drumming hooves.

She threw back the sheet and slipped out of bed. Her shadow followed her across the floorboards as she felt her way past the chamber pot which her father had bought at auction when Alderman Turbill moved to Adelaide, around the side-table that she had decorated with ribbons and fabrics and her own mirror – egg-shaped with a silver border from which dangled a spare handbag, inherited from her grandmother – to the window. Her first impulse after widening the latch – to gulp in the air. It had the whiff of saltbush, and was a reminder of how the night's smells were stranger than the day's, and had more in common with the baying that challenged her from beyond the mullock.

Every time Rosalind looked out of the bedroom which she had shared with William until his death three years ago, and since then with her younger sister Lizzie – burbling to herself in her sleep in the parallel narrow bed – there, 600 yards away, loomed the mullock. It hung over the town like an enormous slouch hat, throwing out a long, unwelcome shadow.

Ordinarily, the gigantic heap of tippings would have been a barrier to check Rosalind's roving thoughts. But her thoughts were not obedient. She peered into the black shape that it cast, and felt a dizzying tug. As if the mullock was clutching out to unite her shadow with its own.

Rosalind had climbed it often enough in daylight – with Oliver, and before that with William. From the top, Broken Hill could clearly be seen in miniature below.

She saw herself gazing down through the smoking shaft-heads: on her parents' bungalow in Rakow Street, the yard with the dairy cows and wrecked buggy, over the galvanised rooftops and humpies of North Broken Hill, over the water-tanks perched on angle-iron towers as if ready to stride off, over the dust cloud raised by a string of camels, across a red sandy loam covered with saltbush and bluebush, mile after mile, to Silverton. This was the extent and bound of her world, sandwiched between the Umberumberka Creek in Silverton, where dawn was appearing over the dry and dreary tableland in – what had he called it? – two bullock hides of light, and the slag-heap that frowned over every street.

Her idea of the universe was indeed wretched. The only break in the drip-drip of the days was the train.

Sydney was a distance of 1446 miles by railway, and it cost as much to travel there by train – on a roundabout route through Adelaide, Melbourne and Albury – as to London by ship. Most likely, she would live to see the ocean only in a mirage.

Rosalind's shadow on the striped wallpaper showed the nightdress pulling tight across her breasts.

She had felt rebellious since William was taken away. His death made her afraid of everything and nothing.

Her fingers squeezed the latch till they hurt. All these stupid questions about who she was going to marry. Come to your senses, Rosalind. And her whispered words in the dark produced a shudder in the bed behind.

Suddenly, she wanted to vanish. Not to be here, in this room, with her shadow on the wall and Lizzie moaning, as she always did when her bladder was full – Rosalind had already woken her sister twice and helped her onto the chamber pot.

In their grief, their parents seemed to have forgotten Lizzie's complications. She had become Rosalind's responsibility. But however much Rosalind loved her little sister, she longed to leave.

If she could change place with one of those stars.

Like them, Rosalind felt fully formed. She knew her mind. She knew everything came hard, what the price of everything was in Stack & Tyndall's drapery store, where she stood behind the counter. She could envisage her future with Oliver. It did not need much imagining. Even Lizzie could have drawn it in one of her episodes of normality.

She moved and her shadow moved. Other women kept telling her that she had a good figure. Rosalind dared not contemplate what that meant.

Still gripping the latch, she leaned forward, tossed by another thought: his rough fingers touching her, thudding into her every night.

Her thoughts bucked and she held on tight. It was terrible to be in this state of disarray.

The stars glittered in the water-trough outside

11

the Freiberg Arms Hotel and on the railway behind. Her eyes picked out the iron tracks and followed them – past the garden fences, towards the Picton sale-yard. The rails curved beside the trench containing the wooden stave water-pipe to Silverton.

The train was the only way out. Either that, or you plunged into the earth.

In William's day, she would have expected to see a long line of men walking like all miners in the world, heads lowered, ready to descend into darkness. This morning, Rakow Street stretched deserted and silent. The mines had been working half-time since August. The presence on the pavements, and in the bars and boarding-houses, of so many unemployed single men with no hope of work, save as soldiers, was unsettling. Miss Pollock had taught that the Aborigines named the district Willyama, meaning Youth. Once upon a time, this was a town of prospectors looking for lodes, and finding them. Now, there was nothing for a young person to do in Broken Hill, except die or leave. Or sail to Suez.

Oliver was one of the fortunate ones, earning twenty-six shillings for three shifts a week. He was twenty-seven and had come from Melbourne ten years before, at the urging of his uncle, Clarence Dowter, to assist him in the laying of the water-pipe. He had stayed on, doing various jobs, until he was offered a position in the South Mine, working in the same team as her brother.

Soon, he would be climbing out of bed in his rented room in Piper Street. Rosalind saw him soaping his nose and face, washing the smoke and fumes off him and his musty carbide smell, and putting on his suit for the Oddfellows' picnic. And before he locked his door and strolled over to Tom Blows's garage and then to Alf Fiddaman's grocery store, slipping that gold-bound opal into the pocket of his flannel shirt.

She felt a hostage to her parents' expectations. Oliver was the life they wished for her. Rosalind's mother in particular.

Rosalind was lucky to have attracted an admirer, was her mother's opinion. Emmy Filwell had lost her son to the mine; her youngest daughter to the water on her brain. With more girls than boys in Broken Hill, she wanted Rosalind settled.

Encouraged by Mrs Filwell, steadily and persistently Oliver had been at her, trying to get her to say yes.

What would William have thought?

Oliver was with her brother in the South Mine on that November night, three years ago. They were popping rocks 825 feet below the surface, when

William crawled away on his hands and knees, and Oliver heard him say, 'I can't find it along here,' then heard a sound like something falling, and on crawling after him discovered that his mate had tumbled down a winze sixty feet deep, fracturing his skull.

Oliver had helped to compose the lines they had put in the *Barrier Miner*:

> *Do not ask us if we miss him,*
> *There is such a vacant place;*
> *Can we e'er forget his footsteps,*
> *And his dear, familiar face?*

He had never been able to explain to her what, precisely, William had been looking for, in the dark, on his hands and knees.

Oliver, called Ollie by all who knew him (but not by Rosalind), had her brother's hands and fingernails. A practical man, with a box of second-hand tools, he could repair an electric motor with his eyes shut, or a radiator hose, or a blocked pipe beneath the sink, and in his spare time was vice-captain of the Broken Hill rugby team and secretary of the local rifle club.

Who never hid his delight when he saw Rosalind.

She enjoyed her power over him. Under pressure from her mother, she had started to put aside money that she earned from the drapery store towards their future together. Oliver Goodmore at least offered an escape from the morbidity of the Filwell household and the nagging responsibility of her sister.

Oliver was good with Lizzie. He was natural with her, and patient, and never laughed when she was silly. Rosalind liked that.

Then she saw in him a kindness that pleased her.

He was different from his friends, who always had one too many. He had flashes of intelligence and tenderness, and was ready to help others. He was quite authoritarian, although he could hold that in check if he wanted to be nice. When he wanted to be nice, he gave her the full battery of his attention.

Rosalind was thinking about this when there was a movement at the corner of Garnet Street. The street was not empty after all. She watched a thin horse lumber out of the mullock's shadow, drawing behind it a white cart.

The cart glistened like a patch of silver as it came creaking down the far side of the road. She craned forward. Two men were seated side by side under the canopy. They were dark-skinned, and beneath their open khaki coats wore red jackets, and on their heads white turbans. The tails of the turbans trailed over their shoulders.

They made a strange contrast in the starlight. The old man, short and fat, sitting with his arms folded; the younger, slim, also clean-shaven but taller, slapping the reins. And above them, the pyramidical shape of the mullock.

The configurations of the night were inexplicable as her sister's madness. The old man seemed to have twinkling rings on his fingers and toes.

As if Rosalind had murmured 'Stop!' the horse pulled over and started drinking from the water trough opposite. Only then did she recognise the younger man – Gül Mehmet. She had never seen Gül in a turban.

The portly old man seemed familiar, too, except that he had shaved off the grey forked beard which she recalled scrolling over his pot-belly.

Rosalind tilted her head. But their conversation was inaudible above whatever Lizzie was now tittering about in her sleep, like the giggles that other children burst into on seeing her.

With reluctance, Rosalind turned from the window. She would have to wake up her sister so that she didn't wet her bed.

The two men had ridden out that morning from the North Camel Camp at the extreme end of Williams

Street. The camp consisted of a few galvanised sheds surrounded by a loose wire fence. There was a small brick building with a tin roof that served as a mosque, and two struggling rows of date palms. Here lived thirty or so camel drivers, mostly Afghans and Indians, with their families and animals.

The settlement had been there since 1890 and was resented by a minority in Broken Hill, who nicknamed it 'Ghantown'. Their prejudice found its mouthpiece in a former editor of the *Barrier Miner*, Ralph Axtell, who though living for some years in Melbourne had returned to Broken Hill a fortnight before to visit a sick cousin. The Benevolent Society, on hearing that Axtell planned to remain in town until after Christmas, had invited him to give an end-of-the-year address. This had taken place the previous evening at the Trades Hall on Blende Street.

Being New Year's Eve, many Benelovent Society members chose to remain at home with their families. But the poor size of the audience, patchily spread out over the three front rows, failed to douse Axtell or the fervour of his delivery. Those who attended his talk, including a reporter from his old newspaper, listened intently to what he had to say.

A nuggety socialist with a high forehead and a thick ginger moustache, Axtell transformed when on stage into a dynamic orator. He was a skilled agitator against Afghans and other 'Turkey lollies', as he called them. His fiery lecture was a get-together of his old saws, and calculated to fan the anti-Turk feeling which had re-emerged since the outbreak of war. The target of his scorn was the posturing German Kaiser, but Axtell went further to include the Ottoman Sultan and Caliph, Mehmet V, who that summer had signed a treaty with the Germans; then to encompass all Muslims, who were said to regard the Sultan as their leader; before homing in on those who lived just up the road, 'in that smellful spot known as Ghantown'.

Axtell reminded his listeners that he had nothing against the foreigner – provided he joined a union and was a white man. Axtell's particular gripe was with the Afghans, as many in the room might recall. Ten years earlier he had stood in this very hall and warned that if the citizens of Broken Hill did not crush the Afghan, the Afghan would crush them. Nothing since had induced Axtell to alter his opinion. These 'Ram Chundahs' and 'Hooshtas' were dangerous. They were bound by their faith to respond to the call to jihad that the Sultan had announced in November – being sympathetically disposed towards those whom Broken Hill's sons, husbands and brothers were, he said, 'even at this moment battling with their lives'.

Axtell looked around. He saw a history of fear overlaid with hate in the faces below. Gazing up at him were snow-bearded veterans who had fought in the Boer War, as well as anti-war miners who marched in protest to the Sulphide Street station, their band playing 'The Internationale' while they themselves hooted and booed recruits departing for the Ascot Park training camp in Adelaide.

In a quiet, suddenly insinuating voice, Axtell reassured his small audience: 'Self-preservation is the first law of nature.' Whatever one's opinions on the conflict in Europe – as a good socialist Axtell had plenty – the entire sympathy of the nation ought to be with the White Australia policy.

At this, several aldermen in the front row muttered 'Hear, hear', and Clarence Dowter, seated beside his nephew, began nodding.

'The Afghans have taken our jobs,' Axtell went on. They were brutal and depraved. And filthy in their daily habits. Even the Aboriginals found them unacceptable! In only the short time that Axtell had been back in Broken Hill, he had learned that it was almost impossible for residents to live near the camel camp, due to the nauseating stench from the decomposing entrails of dead animals thrown out by the inhabitants.

Axtell concluded by suggesting that the time had come to expel the Afghans and that a new Citizen Vigilance Committee be formed against this Asiatic canker, of which the Afghan presented the most visible sign – 'with that diabolical grin of dissimulation which of all people he possesses to perfection'. He called for a show of hands.

Next to Oliver, his uncle's arm flew up, as did the arms of Oliver's mates in the rifle club – young men like Roy Sleath, the policeman's son; Alf Fiddaman, the grocer; and Tom Blows, a friendly, round-faced lad with jug ears who worked for the Water Pipe Company. Even old Ern Pilkinghorne, though deaf, raised his hand after a moment. Eyes sunk in his narrow head, and with his white beard neatly trimmed, Ern had not heard a word, but he liked to attend these meetings; the sight of so many enthralled faces was a solace.

Emboldened by their example, Oliver, who had come here at the last moment at Tom Blows's request, lifted his hand into the air. Even so, Axtell's speech made him uncomfortable. It untethered emotions, suspicions and latent jealousies which he would have preferred to stay unaroused.

To meet the cost of his engagement ring, Oliver had put his name down for the half-shift on New Year's Eve; he was not due at the mine until 10 pm. Instead of going back to Cobalt Street with Tom Blows, who wanted him to take a look at his motorbike – he complained it was back-firing – Oliver had called at Rosalind's house. He had decided to ask her to marry him at the Oddfellows' picnic next day. But time was running out. Before he could propose, he first needed to secure Mr Filwell's permission – something that Oliver had been planning to do earlier in the week, until some camels intervened.

The light was growing stale in the sky, the last sunset of the year. Oliver walked in a loping gait up Blende Street and slowed as he approached the Filwell bungalow. Perhaps to calm himself, he started singing a music hall song that he had learned from William.

Rosalind was with her mother in the kitchen, slicing tomatoes, when she heard him.

'Listen . . .' said her mother, straightening her matronly body. She was still waiting for William to return, and he didn't.

Instead, it was Oliver's baritone which competed with the chop of steel on wood.

In her little handsome bonnet, and her cotton dress,
She's as fine as any lass of high degree . . .

From his chair in the green-papered living room, her father called out, 'Open the door for Ollie.' His voice travelled easily through the house.

A pink-faced man with a grey moustache, Albert Filwell always looked stern and angry, even when he was laughing. Yet William's death had crushed him. Soon after his son's accident, he had given up mines for cows; and twice a week he taught the Broken Hill Brigade boys how to shoot. But his self-esteem had rotted.

Towards Oliver, he behaved with a complicated hostility. He knew that he should support the young man's courtship of his daughter. It was a link to his son, like the song.

Rosalind wiped her hands on her apron and went to let Oliver in.

'Get us something to drink, would you, Ros?' her father said, after she had ushered Oliver into the living room.

She brought in two glasses and a bottle of ginger beer, and returned to the kitchen, promising to be back once she'd finished preparing the picnic. She and her mother were making mutton sandwiches with tomatoes and lettuce, and a lamington cake. Oliver had already volunteered to bring fruit.

With exaggerated care, Oliver poured out the ginger beer. He felt doubly grateful to be left alone with Rosalind's father. Quite apart from the matter they needed to discuss, Albert Filwell would be a dependable sounding board for the turbulent feelings that Ralph Axtell had stirred up.

Filwell winced as he raised his elbow to take the glass. 'Rosalind tell you what happened?'

Oliver sat down and slapped his pockets for his pipe. 'Your horse went berserk, right?'

'I'll say she did.'

His right arm swaying in a sling, Filwell was eager to go over it again, how his horse broke its tackling when it encountered a camel-string heading towards Ghantown. His milk buggy – damaged beyond even Oliver's capacity to repair it – had overturned, and he was jolted from his seat, falling heavily to the ground.

Through the thin partition, Rosalind could hear him saying, 'I was howling the place down, I tell you. I was groaning worse than a foundered mule. Dr Large sent me off to the bloody hospital. On Boxing Day!'

She opened the oven and peered in at the sponge. Her father never talked to her like this. Her thoughts were to be confined to the kitchen, patted and kneaded into the same standard shapes, and put into the oven and baked.

In the next room, Filwell continued to air his grievance. His mare had every right to go berserk. Camels were evil creatures, with their agonising bray. Eating the bush and polluting the water-holes. 'I'd like to put a bullet in the lot of them!'

Rosalind took this in, grimly, as she pressed into the sponge to see if it would spring back: *a horse goes berserk at the sight of a camel. A camel goes berserk at the sound of a cockatoo. We all go mad at something,* and slid back the pan. *Even a rabbit bouncing past can start off the cows.*

'Now, Rosalind, a kitchen isn't for standing in.' Grief had made her mother snappy. She held her dimpled arms around a bundle of clothes. 'Why don't you wash that lettuce while you're waiting?' and opened the door and went out.

Oliver's voice came through the wall. She could hear every word. 'Do you know the owner?'

'Oh, I reckon,' said Rosalind's father. The chair creaked as he rocked back. 'It's that butcher fella. The one your uncle keeps taking to court.'

'Those Afghans and their bloody oonts.'

And Rosalind pictured Oliver scowling as he excavated with a thick index finger the scorched bowl of his pipe.

Before he found work in the South Mine, Oliver had earned his living as a woodcutter. Then the Afghans had arrived and raided all the firewood for fifty miles around. Just as they'd moved in on the striking shearers and displaced the bullock and horse teamsters. If his uncle didn't make a stand to defend the butchers, it wouldn't be long before the Afghans took all the butchers' jobs too.

'You know what the trouble is, Mr Filwell?' For a moment, Oliver assumed the union-leader's tone of his uncle. 'People don't speak up. When I don't like someone, I say what I think, and I don't like the Afghans.' He read the papers, but he never read anything that had an explanation for why they should be here. 'All I know is that I don't cadge, Mr Filwell. And I claim the right to object to cadgers in any shape.'

Rosalind's father tilted forward on the chair-scratched lino, fighting his slight aversion to Oliver. 'I'm with you there,' raising his glass with his unaffected arm. His lips clamped down on his mouthful of ginger beer, and there was a loud noise as he swallowed it.

To Rosalind, all her father's restraint and fortitude seemed to have disappeared at the memory of his collision with Molla Abdullah's camel-train – Oliver's as well. She had never before heard Oliver speak with such spite. Was this what he believed in his heart? She picked up the lettuce that Alf Fiddaman had let her have cheap, and peered at it for dirt.

But Oliver had not finished. What upset him more was the way that Afghans looked at white women. Exactly as Afghan competition had killed off the woodcutters, the teamsters and other white jobs, so were white women in danger, Oliver believed.

Rosalind felt her heart speed up. A slug was wiggling its way deep into the lettuce. She picked it out and flicked it into the sink – only to be trapped by a recent memory of looking on hypnotised at Oliver's big, stumpy, confident hands as he sorted out the blockage in the pipe beneath.

'I'm not just talking about Sukey.'

Rosalind inclined her head until it touched the weatherboard partition. Mary Brodribb, back in January, had told her about Sukey, a tall, bony girl who rode in on a grey horse and charged ten shillings for twenty minutes behind a blanket that she draped over a branch.

'Other white women, too, get involved with them.'

Did Oliver have Gül in mind? Did he have *her* in mind? She wondered with panic if Mary might have spoken to him.

Oliver laid it out like Axtell. Young Australian women who should know better stood hanging about the camel camp. Something attracted them. And some could end up getting into trouble, married even . . .

So Oliver and her father peddled stories of disease, dirt and depravity. To Rosalind, overhearing and unable to pull herself away, it was dreadful what they said in their low ridiculing voices. It was as if something about the uncivilised and disgusting Afghan provoked a fear that ran deeper than any shaft in the South Mine. She wished they'd stop it.

Through the partition, she listened as Oliver said in a different voice, 'Something else I'd like to talk to you about.'

Her pulse was beating as she angled her ear against the wall to hear more, but her mother was calling from the yard for Rosalind to take the sponge out of the oven.

Making cakes was all her mother knew how to do after William died, and she had not discovered how to stop. William had appreciated her cakes – more so than Rosalind. Of his sisters, only Lizzie shared his sweet tooth.

The door opened.

'Should I use jam for the icing?' Her mother in a clay-coloured cardigan stood staring at Rosalind.

'You know I don't like jam,' said Rosalind. '*Or* cake.'

'This cake isn't for you.'

'Who's it for, then?'

Stout with depression and with shoulders sunk, her mother walked across the floor of the kitchen to the cupboard, holding her arms away from her side, as if carrying two heavy metal pails filled with the washing that she took in to earn extra money.

Suddenly, Rosalind was all directness. 'It's not going to bring him back, mother. He's gone. He'll never eat another of your cakes.'

'Well, Ollie likes jam.' Her face defiant.

Rosalind gave a harsh laugh. 'He's called Oliver. You're not his mother. You're not his mother-in-law, either,' and untied her apron and flung it onto the kitchen table.

Seconds later, Rosalind strode into the living room. 'What have you two been gabbing about?' looking from her father, who had a strange embarrassed expression as if he wanted to let her into a secret, to Oliver, who stood with his back to the fireplace, smiling.

'If it's not Rosalind,' said Oliver, concentrating on his pipe, as on the occasion when he came home late with William, eyes not meeting hers, but proud of something he had seen or done. (It turned out he'd been scrawling 'scab' on a grave.)

She crossed the room in a perversely springy walk and spread her hands on the back of her father's chair. She breathed heavily. 'Aren't you going to tell me?'

In the kitchen, the jam cupboard opened and closed. Her father seemed compressed into his twitching arm. The only sound, the helpless clock on the papered wall.

Oliver tapped out his pipe against the empty hearth. 'Well, goodnight, Mr Filwell. I'm pleased we've got that sorted. I'd better get down to the poppet head.' And in the hallway, 'Goodnight, Mrs Filwell! I hope that sink's still behaving itself!' And in a voice that he tried to make softer to Rosalind, who had opened the front door for him, 'Goodnight, you.'

He stood under the fluted glass lily shade and looked into her eyes, as if she was now available to him and he had some sway over her. 'I'll see you at the train station at ten, then,' touching her arm. 'Tom's asked me to take a squiz at his motorbike. If I'm late . . .'

Rosalind found her smile and kissed him quickly on the cheek. 'I'll keep a place for you.' Her arm was all tense, waiting for him to leave.

He tried to slam the door shut from the outside, but she was still holding the handle.

Rosalind listened to him walking off. He was singing to himself, the only song he knew.

She's a pretty liddle girl from nowhere . . .

One slow step at a time, she made her way back to the living room. Her father sat looking at her.

She brushed a grey wisp of hair away from his ears. Picked up the bottle. 'More?'

'I'm doing very well,' draining his glass and handing it to her.

She held the empty glass against her chest.

His face had taken on a weight, as if charged with some mineral. 'You been arguing with your mother again?' And when she didn't reply, 'Ros . . . I don't . . . Is something wrong?' suddenly intimate, as though he had a vision of Oliver Goodmore prising the glass from her fingers. Then of Oliver unbuttoning her pale blue blouse. Touching her high young breasts . . .

He raised his injured arm, and stretched out to Rosalind, so that she smelled the Chamberlain's Pain Balm which she had rubbed into his bruised elbow two hours earlier.

His sling was beginning to smell, too.

'I can't describe it,' she said, resisting his invitation to hug her. 'It's just . . .' And wriggled her shoulders as if something was crawling there.

Opposite Rosalind's window, the horse finished drinking. The cart clopped on, following the railway line towards the Picton sale-yard. She could see the two men still engaged in conversation. They must be up this early in order to reach Silverton in time for the picnic. Gül would need to be selling his ice-creams before the sun grew too angry.

Rosalind had encountered Gül eight days earlier, at the town's Christmas Eve dance in the Trades Hall. He stood inside the vestibule with two other dark-skinned young men.

Lizzie stared back at him through eyes lazy and narrowed. Her face in her outsized head had the energy of an unformed sentence.

'Ros,' she rejoiced, 'look what I see.'

Rosalind remembered the way Oliver turned his long nose in the men's direction, his annihilating glance.

'Camel-li-as,' he said. He pronounced the word with a lilt before the third and fourth syllables, as if he could already sniff the strong camel odour.

'What?' It was Rosalind's turn to say something, indignant over that 'Camel-li-as'.

'From Ghantown.'

Rosalind knew where they were from. She wanted to ask Gül about the injury to his hand. But he was being restrained from entering by a suddenly superior-looking Roy Sleath.

Something in Gül's expression continued to hold Rosalind. He wore European clothes, and stood straight and tall.

'Strike me pink,' said Oliver, puffing up his cheeks like a bugler. 'Isn't that Lakovsky's Turkey lolly?'

But she was not revolted by him as Oliver seemed to demand.

Nor Lizzie.

Her sister was chewing her knuckles and looking into his hurt dark eyes. He was refusing to budge.

'Alf will help see them off,' Oliver decided, and called over to a stoutish young man with a wart on his eyebrow.

'Shall I ask him to dance?' Lizzie enquired, and kicked out her legs in a crude jig. She had no sense of her effect on others.

'No,' ordained Oliver in a cavalierish voice, 'you will dance with me.'

Arm-in-arm, he escorted Lizzie through the packed hall towards the stage where a brass band was beginning to play.

Leaving Rosalind standing there.

Meanwhile, Alf Fiddaman, who could be a bit of a hothead, was aping the Germans' marching style and thrusting the three Afghans back towards the entrance with Roy Sleath's assistance. 'Sorry, camel-lips!'

Rosalind was conscious of a savage intensification of feeling. Gül seemed to look at her, before raising his hand – still wrapped in her handkerchief. It was a small gesture, but remembered to exaggeration by Rosalind as some sort of farewell.

Then, without resistance, he turned and walked out.

She thought of Gül next day when her father shooed away a small group of Afghan children who stood hopefully on the doorstep in their best clothes, asking to be allowed to join in the family's Christmas celebrations.

One girl, braver than the rest, with paler skin, stood her ground. 'Please, mister.'

'You please yourself what you do, but if you ever come round here again you won't walk away from the place.'

The choppy pitch of his voice upset Rosalind, and she made the mistake of saying so in front of her sister. 'After all, local European children are welcome at the Ramadan feast.'

'How do you know?' said Lizzie, stepping out of

her slow churn of thought. She unwound her glance from the drawing she was doing of the crocodile she had always believed lived under her bed, and looked up at Rosalind. 'Ros, you haven't been hanging about there, have you?'

She had, but she did not reveal this to Lizzie. Her younger sister was the last person she would have told.

A loud explosion eight months earlier had drawn Rosalind to the settlement. A shot in the camp that brought out all the cats and dogs in Williams Street, returning at a run with bits of offal dangling from their jaws. Evidently, they knew when a sick camel was slaughtered.

She had been on her way to the Brodribbs' house, to lend Mary a novel she'd borrowed from the free lending library, and was already in a strangely restless mood. Moments before, she had had an awkward encounter with her former teacher.

An engagement broken off, a Greek-sounding name. Miss Pollock had recently come back to Broken Hill with an orange dress and not much else, after things had not worked out in Adelaide. ('He promised her the earth,' confided Mary, who believed in the infallibility of everything she overheard in Harvey's, even when the speaker was Mrs Rasp, 'then treated her like dirt.') And though Miss Pollock professed chirpily there was no place like home, she hadn't truly returned.

They had stopped on the side of the road. Miss Pollock, who was never at her best in public, started off politely, but soon became oddly inquisitive, asking Rosalind about her life since the last time they had met, almost four years ago, when Rosalind was about to leave school.

'Mrs Stack offered me a position.'

Miss Pollock nodded. A job at 'The People's Drapery' wasn't to be sniffed at, with everyone at the front or being laid off; seventy-five per cent of the population were on half-time.

But her smile was congested.

'And you'll get married,' she said out of her unusually lined face. 'And live here. With your grandchildren.'

Rosalind remembered her grandmother swishing around town in her moss-coloured dress, muttering to herself.

She wanted to say, 'I expect you are right,' but altered this into 'I would like something more'. She looked surprised by the words that blurted from her mouth, as if put there by someone else.

'Something more?'

'Yes. Something more.' Rosalind's voice sounded steely in its surround of politeness.

Miss Pollock gazed at Rosalind. 'There's nothing more,' she said matter-of-factly, and her expression turned to pity. 'You must realise this is an egotistical town, Rosalind. It makes you think of yourself only.'

BANG.

At the sound of the shot, Miss Pollock broke off their conversation, and hurried away.

Rosalind couldn't help being infected by her teacher's mood. She continued along Williams Street, and was less than 100 yards from the Brodribbs' house when she saw a little grey dog, too small for what it had snatched, lie down in the shade and lick its tongue around something large and shiny. As if tugged by an invisible rope, she decided to turn right, towards Ghantown, and see for herself this much talked-about place.

If you don't behave, the Afghans will get you, her father used to joke.

Provoked by her father, and by the picture that one or two of Oliver's mates had painted, but most of all by her unsatisfactory exchange with Miss Pollock, Rosalind walked along the perimeter until she entered the camel camp. She did not know what she would find, or even what she was looking for. Her brother in the dark groped for something he could not see.

And what had she seen?

Square wool bales like wombat dung.

Children returning in a line from school, the boys in turbans, clean white trousers, and black waistcoats with large buttons.

A sockless man at the top of a ladder pollinating the date palms.

From under the trees came a strong, latrine-like stench.

Cross-legged on a tarpaulin, a black-haired young man sat repairing a broken saddle with a packing needle. He did not move his head as she passed.

Further in, camels lay on their stomachs on the flat ground, swinging their lower lips back and forth as they chewed. They looked jittery and somehow different from the creatures that meandered in placid columns beside the road to Silverton. His arm around a camel's neck, fondling its ear, a boy talked soothingly in a foreign language – in Pushtu? – calming them.

The transition exhilarated Rosalind. One moment she was wandering along Williams Street, saying a stilted good afternoon to her old teacher; the next, she could have been standing on the banks of the Nile. It was hardly possible for her two eyes to take it all in.

Bent over under the bough of a white gum, a bare-headed old man with a protruding belly sawed noisily at a carcass. Patriarchal, thick, and divided in two, his grey beard seemed to brush the ground.

Rosalind stood there uncertain, her eyes on this small, stocky butcher who was cutting up the dead camel, in between fending off a pack of darting dogs and cats – until a woman in a veil hurried over and motioned her into a skillion-roofed shed with a hessian partition, no windows but open one end. Old clothes and dried dingo scalps dangled from bent wires, like the hooks that held up her father's horse harness. On a table constructed from packing cases was a jam tin filled with dripping, and a slush lamp with a strip of trouser cloth for wick.

The veiled woman scrubbed out a plate with wet sand, and put onto it something plucked from a box suspended by wires, and indicated that she should eat. Rosalind thanked her. She examined the doughy offering, the depressions with thumb prints, and took a tiny polite bite. The tart, peppery flavour was invigoratingly unlike her mother's johnnycakes.

Rolled out on the ground was a brilliant-coloured rug, embroidered with unfamiliar patterns and motifs. Invited to sit down, Rosalind knelt and looked outside at the camels. She was conscious of the tinkling of bells and of muscles relaxing on arched necks. Also, of the odd way the animals examined her. Miss Pollock had taught that the camel had a membrane like a black film, which in desert storms shut across the eye while the lid remained wide open, to protect it from stinging sand. So Rosalind chewed on her curry-flavoured chapatti and gazed back.

Without the camel, Miss Pollock had told her class in Gypsum Street, *the empty places would never have been opened up at all.*

A goat came in at the entrance and stood and eyed Rosalind, the sand bubbling and darkening around its hind legs. Under the white gum, the long-bearded figure went on sawing. She thought of Sukey, who lived wherever night overtook her, and wondered if it was over that branch that Sukey tossed her blanket.

Rosalind had visited the camp once more, at the end of June. A holy man from Sinde was touring the bush mosques. It was Ramadan, and camelmen from miles around had gathered to be within the emanation of this travelling imam whom everyone was talking about.

She was intensely curious to see what a holy man looked like. He was twice descended from the Prophet, the papers said.

When she reached the camel camp: the noise. The

braying and bleating was louder than the town's brass band tuning up. Rosalind was again made welcome. She was given a glass of tea and invited to take her place on a bench where a slender young man who had arrived late was removing his sandals, adding them to a heap. Also milling about were children whose faces she recognised – Prisks, Rutts, Spanglers, Deebles. Their families lived in the neighbouring streets.

Figures bustled past dressed in white flowing clothes. What Rosalind saw mocked the stories she had heard. These people weren't unclean. She was surprised by how exceptionally clean, in fact, they were. Her mother couldn't have laundered their clothes to this standard.

It was made clear to Rosalind that she couldn't join in the prayers, but she managed to eavesdrop. So many worshippers had assembled at the mosque that its door had been wedged open in order for those outside to hear. She peered over their backs into a room about twenty feet long by fifteen feet wide, heavily carpeted, and lit by two lamps. In successive flashes, she catalogued a driftwood stand with an open book resting on it. A bunch of emu feathers on the wall. Two pictures – Mecca? Bethlehem? And lying on the carpet, face up, a circular wood-framed clock that might have come from the railway station.

Glancing from time to time at the clock, the holy man stood leading the prayers. Rosalind's only yardstick for holiness was the Reverend Cornelius Hayball, and the imam did not look like him. He was under average height, sandy complexioned with a white beard, and on his head a bright white turban. He bent and kissed the Koran, then turned the pages from the end, reading passages aloud.

Transfixed, Rosalind watched the lines of worshippers kneel on the prayer mats, touch the ground with their foreheads, then sit back, chanting in unison, '*La-ilaha-illa-Allah wa ashhadu anna Muhammadan abduhu wa rasuluh.*'

A balding assistant with a divided grey beard limped in the imam's wake, a pace or two behind. Rosalind recognised the sawing figure from under the gum tree. And then it came to her where on another occasion she had seen this man: he had helped shovel away the sand after the dust storm in January.

That storm was one of the most violent anyone could recall, announced by dark specks tumbling high overhead – twigs, bones and other detritus blown into the upper atmosphere by fierce currents of wind, and far in advance of the angry tube of grey smoke that rolled across the horizon from east to west. She and Lizzie had raced inside to block all keyholes, windows and fireplaces. For four days, red-brown dust and gravel had rattled down on the iron roof in Rakow Street, blocking out the sun. By the time the storm passed on to the Mallee, their house was buried up to its bargeboards. The cameleers had had to bring along the scoop which they used for excavating water catchments. They had worked for hours. And this bald fat man with the long forked beard and a limp had been their foreman.

Otherwise, she looked around at men who were physically imposing and graceful in their movements. Rosalind also saw one white woman with five children.

All this occurred in June. She met Gül nearly five months later, in the second week of November. She had finished her afternoon shift at the drapery store and was walking home when she heard a clang.

The white-painted cart on which he sat shaking a cowbell caught her attention more than Gül. It was hitched to a thin bay horse with its head in a nosebag, and was low-sided like her grandmother's four-poster bed – so that Rosalind's first thought was of her grandmother, stalking through the dust in a tattered dress, after losing her savings to a lanky hawker of bogus mine shares that she had purchased under the balcony of the Denver City Hotel.

Rosalind waited until the steam tram had passed, then stepped closer. The four barley-sugar posts supported a dark green tarpaulin to shade the ice-cream chest in the back.

She read the words italicised on the side of the cart.

Lakovsky's Delicious ITALIAN ICE CREAM. A Food fit for Children and Invalids.

She was about to cross the street when he called out in surprisingly good English, 'Warn your children against inferior vendors!'

'I don't have children,' and looked at him. Dressed in waistcoat and watch.

Was he one of those sitting back on his heels outside the mosque? He had given her the excuse to stare, at least. He wore loose blue dungarees tied at the ankle and under his waistcoat an oversize bushman's shirt that hung down over his trousers. One of his boots had no lace.

She felt her face colouring. 'Are you new to Broken Hill?' for something to say. She had never before seen this two-wheeled cart.

But he was not to be pinned down so easily. 'Prompt delivery and general satisfaction is my motto.'

At this, Rosalind couldn't help smiling. She recognised his manager's words.

'Does that mean Mr Lakovsky's freezer is working again?'

Leo Lakovsky was a Russian Jew from Odessa who advertised himself as 'Broken Hill's No. 1 champion ice-cream manufacturer'. He recently had imported an expensive freezer from America, powered by electric motor. But less than a week after he installed it at his premises in Blende Street, the famous electric motor had broken down. Distraught, Lakovsky had summoned Oliver Goodmore. The machine needed to be mended if the Russian wasn't to have his licence taken away by the town's overzealous sanitary inspector, Oliver's uncle, Clarence Dowter.

'Oh, it bin working very well.' The bell was put down and he swivelled. From one of the tubs inside the chest, he scraped out a spoonful of ice-cream.

He turned back, lifting it for her to taste.

'Buttermilk ice. Only four per cent fat. Most delicious.'

The sun was shining. His hands, she saw, were clean.

Shyness prevented her from knowing what to do.

'I'm . . .' ruffled by a gust that no one else in Argent Street seemed to be feeling.

She knew the person who had repaired the freezer. She could tell him that. Or that Oliver was twisting

44

Lakovsky's arm to favour Rosalind's father as the chief supplier of his milk, in place of that larrikin Beek who wasn't a member of the Milk Vendors' Association.

'Go on, taste.'

The ice-cream was beginning to drip down his fingers.

'Where are you from?' she asked.

'Broken Hill.'

'But before that.'

His chin rose. 'Afghanistan.'

As she opened her mouth, Rosalind was conscious of his eyes on her. They were clear and clean. Like his hand.

And gave a cry that Oliver must have heard over in the South Mine.

She reeled back, choking. What she was recoiling from were two strands of wool. She had swallowed one. She produced the other from her mouth – damp, long, scarlet-coloured – and held it out between her fingers.

How quickly he sprang up, like a sitting camel bounding to its feet. He was new in the job, he apologised. He couldn't imagine how this wool . . . how it could have got itself into the ice-cream.

He snatched the offending strand from her, and insisted that she sample another spoonful from a different tub. And ran around to fetch it, this time yellow in colour and more generous than before.

She tightened her mouth.

He was standing beside her, holding up the spoon.

What had started in fun had become serious. Rosalind no longer had any desire to taste Mr Lakovsky's most delicious buttermilk ice-cream. What she ought to do, she knew, was walk off. But she felt sorry for him. This strange man, the lost foreigner away from his family, ice-cream in the heat, dripping down his fingers.

'All right,' she relented. 'But you can't object if I take a closer look.'

She examined his second offering. Which did on this occasion seem hairless.

After all, well, they were probably only shaken from some rug, and gingerly pushed out her tongue.

'That's the stuff,' in his English from Lakovsky.

It was icy cold, like a blast.

What was the flavour? She was curious to know.

'Pineapple,' his smile growing now.

'How much?'

'Threepence.'

She drew in her breath. There was the smell of hot canvas.

'All right, I'll buy one.'

Rosalind fished around in her purse while he filled a cone. 'I've got sixpence only,' giving him the coin, and in the same motion taking his ice-cream.

He looked crestfallen – he didn't have change. Mrs Rasp had used up his last pennies with her sovereign.

It was suddenly all very irritating. 'Keep the sixpence,' she told him. He could bring it to her later, what he owed. She worked at Stack & Tyndall's. 'I will be there tomorrow.' And the day after, she said to herself.

It was easier than returning the cone.

'But who do I ask for?' he said.

Her hazel eyes looked at him. 'Rosalind Filwell.'

'Rosalind Filwell, I will see you tomorrow.' There was nothing casual about his promise or about the way he spoke her name.

'I am Gül Mehmet.'

The following afternoon in the drapery store, Mrs Rasp tried on a straw bonnet on which Mrs Stack had reduced the price. She planted her feet apart to assess herself in the floor-length mahogany mirror. Her flat white face was an envelope, but with nothing inside unless a thank-you letter from the League of the Helping Hand. She should stop trying to convince people she was not a whale, thought Rosalind.

With a toss of her head, as though a young woman again, Mrs Rasp addressed Rosalind in the glass. 'Do you imagine you'll be here, behind that counter, for the next twelve years? Looking at people like me in the mirror? Don't you have other ambitions?'

'I don't know.'

Mrs Rasp contemplated Rosalind's breasts, which always aggravated her, and the accumulated years tumbled back. 'There are good shops in Adelaide. You could always try,' she said in a distant voice. She rotated her plump body, and laid the bonnet on the counter. 'I'll take it.'

Mrs Rasp had left Stack & Tyndall's by the time Gül Mehmet appeared in the doorway. His glance ricocheted around the store – tablecloths suspended from the ceiling; hats on wooden stalks, like planets on an orrery; the petticoats, stockings and brassieres – and dropped to the floor.

After a moment of indecision, he advanced in long strides and placed a threepence on the counter, then withdrew his hand.

Mrs Stack sat out of sight in the millinery room, talking in a loud voice to Ern Pilkinghorne about that day's headlines in the *Barrier Miner*. The Ottoman

Empire was being mentioned. And something about a Holy War.

'Of course, the Huns are behind it!' shouted Ern, who had seen action in the Eastern Transvaal with the Victorian Mounted Rifles.

Gül turned to listen, but the news from Europe was getting muffled in the bonnets and a large notice which read: 'If you're not one of our clients, we're both losers.'

His eyes found hers. He asked if she knew what was going on. Had the Allied armies reached Turkey?

Rosalind confessed that she hadn't been following events. She sympathised with Mrs Brodribb, who only the night before had said to her, 'It's too depressing the news, so I listen to music.'

Gül talked about the war for a while. Four of his friends had enlisted with the Expeditionary Forces. They'd left by train last week. He referred to the Gurkhas' bravery in the fighting in Europe. He seemed to take great interest in the fighting.

But his manner had altered from the previous afternoon. He was agitated about something. He looked at Rosalind with a brownish hawk's eye that tore through her. 'Why so many go to war?' he asked, no longer in Lakovsky English.

She pointed outside. 'They want to go. They want

to leave. There's nothing much doing here.'

In the street, a woman was shouting at a small boy.

He had not followed her hand. '*We* are here.' He said it with a laugh.

Her eyes sparkled back in irony. 'Yes, we are. But don't you reckon that says more about us.'

He looked at her reprovingly. 'You believe we enemies?'

'Enemies?' Then, not wishing to be evasive, 'How do you mean, enemies?' and raised the back of her hand to her mouth to suppress a cough.

'What you bin say to him?' He threw the question at her.

'Who?'

His eyes were darker. 'Meester Dowtah. You bin spoke to him!'

'Mr Dowter?' She looked back up, and her body rose and fell.

'He bin say ice-cream dirty. He say I pay fine.' It was all coming out now, in his husky voice. He was angry as two sticks. 'He bin say – oh, why you tell him?'

Hearing voices, Mrs Stack appeared. 'Rosalind, is everything all right?' Sometimes in Stack & Tyndall's someone wanted more than a hat.

'Yes, yes.'

When she turned round, he had gone.

In fact, Rosalind had said nothing to Clarence Dowter about what had made her cry out. The one person she had told, and not in a serious way, was her best friend, Mary Brodribb. That was in the Red Cross Society tea-room in Argent Street.

Now, without quite knowing why, she sought Mary out after work. Had Mary mentioned the story to anyone? She was struck cold to discover she had, only that morning – to Oliver, of all people.

Mary had repeated it to Oliver in Harvey's as he pondered which ring to select from the black velvet tray he had asked her to pull out for him.

Because, Rosalind accepted with a small smile, this is what you did in a place that wasn't even on the edge of things, but in the centre of nowhere. A hole in the earth, and beside it a heap of earth, and no neighbours for hundreds of miles, and those neighbours that you were fortunate to have all of a sudden now in Egypt. So when someone walked into Harvey's – a person who had a jokey way of looking at you that made you feel you were funny and intelligent – to detain them in the jeweller's a moment longer, you ended up glancing over their shoulder at a brass bell clanging and a white cart clattering by. And then leaning forward, cheeks between two hands, you told them about a spoonful of buttermilk ice-cream with something revolting concealed in it, and even quoting Rosalind's words: 'It looked like a red worm!'

It was clear that Oliver had felt obliged to report the matter to his uncle.

And something else Rosalind learned from Mary. 'That engagement ring was for you, Ros!'

Rosalind wished that she had been able to respond with a better smile. After Mary confided in a voice from which she could not keep her envy that she knew where – and when – Ollie was intending to slip the gold-framed opal on Rosalind's finger, Rosalind did not see Oliver on his knees in Umberumberka Creek, but the two black beaks of Gül's eyes tearing at her.

For the rest of that day, Rosalind could not shake off her concern that Gül had suffered all because of something she had told Mary in a giggle over a late biscuit. Clarence Dowter was such a stickler for the rules.

In any case, the way ahead was not so clear or exciting as Mary imagined. A decision would have to be made. And before that an apology.

*

He came into view at the corner of Sulphide Street, shaking his brass cowbell. From a long way off she could make out the green canopy shading the ice-chest, and the cart like the four-poster. She saw her parents on it, on the street in the brutal light.

But when Rosalind waved at him, as if hoping to make reparation by her display of recognition, he gave her an offended stare and urged his horse on, kicking so hard against the cart that his left boot fell off.

He had to jump down and retrieve it.

Rosalind didn't see Gül again for two more days in which she was conscious of her revolving passions. Part of her hoped he hadn't noticed that she cared. But she caught herself scouting the streets and shop-fronts for a pale bay horse, listening out for his bell. The Afghan had started to become interesting now that she had hurt him.

A mistake had been made. She had made it. But it annoyed Rosalind that Oliver had not said a word to her. Wasn't it her story to tell? Definitely, it hadn't been Oliver's to pass on to his uncle behind her back. So when the Sanitary Inspector approached her counter one morning and asked Rosalind to verify an allegation that concerned Gül Mehmet, she gave him a pale smile.

The denial plopped out of her mouth like curdled milk. 'No, it must be a misunderstanding.'

Clarence Dowter had stared at her. 'Are you sure about that?' Everything about him was downturned and suspicious. Her father laughed with his whole frame, but in the case of Oliver's uncle, only his lips moved on the rare occasions when he couldn't conceal his mirth. They were motionless now.

'Quite sure,' said Rosalind cheerfully. 'The ice-cream I had was delicious. It was pineapple.'

'Pineapple?'

'Pineapple. That's right.'

The Sanitary Inspector put his homburg back on and did not thank her for her time.

The Red Cross Society tea-room was in the basement. Rosalind turned around to see if it was Mary descending the metal steps, but it was Mrs Kneeshaw, who gave her a friendly greeting and disappeared into the kitchen. That was when she noticed the woman in the corner. Thirtyish, long blonde hair, with a mole on the side of her nose, like the jewel on an Indian. She sat less than ten feet away, in the shadow of the spiral staircase, stirring her tea.

They caught each other's eye through the cast-iron

banister, and the woman smiled a peculiar smile, then picked up her cup and saucer, and walked over. She wore a long print dress, plum-coloured, and sandals.

'Don't I know you?'

Her gaze did seem familiar.

Now where was it, each one wondered, that they might have met. In the drapery store? The grocery? The Methodist church?

The woman put down her cup, and raised her arm until it was horizontal across her face and the distracting mole. Two green eyes looked over it at Rosalind, as though above a veil. 'Remember now?' and held out her hand.

She seemed thinner than the shrouded woman in blue clustered about with five small children; more angular.

'Sally Khan,' and asked if she could sit down.

Rosalind introduced herself. She had been keeping the chair for a friend. 'But she's late,' she added superfluously.

Sally was intrigued to know what had taken Rosalind to the camel camp.

'I wanted to see if the Afghans would get me,' Rosalind said humorously.

'And did they?'

Rosalind heard herself laugh. 'I'm more worried

about the Australians, to tell the truth.'

Sally cast her an eye of surprised curiosity. 'But you're Australian?'

'I suppose so.' If having two sets of grandparents from Ireland made you Australian.

'How old are you?'

'Twenty-one. Nearly twenty-two.'

'I remember twenty-two . . .' as though it cleared something.

Sally had been that age when she met her first husband in Port Pirie. Alastair. There was a sense of closeness around the wide mouth at his mention. 'He was one of those difficult men. He cared more about his horse than he did about me. With Badsha, I am number one in his life. What did I ever get from Alastair but sneers. It was probably my fault. I did some stupid things. But.'

She laid down her cup with a crack. She was sick to death of Australian men. They were so weak. There was something to be said for an ancient culture. It never made Badsha snaky if she went into town on her own.

Rosalind admired her good humour. Sally seemed to have a happy life, although she did miss her ginger-snaps – and Mrs Kneeshaw's were the best! Which was why Sally liked to pop in to the tea-room when her kids were at school. Only now and then, mind you.

Then she was all apologetic for gabbing on so much. There weren't many Australian women in the camp, and Badsha had no gift for talk. She came here when she wanted to thrash things out in her mind. She thanked Rosalind for being a sympathetic listener. If there was one thing she couldn't bear, it was being told to shut up. 'I don't get to my age to be having someone always yelling at you. Or to be crawling to them for every penny. Badsha gives me half of everything he earns. Like I said, with Badsha I am number one. You're not eating those?'

'Help yourself.'

Sally took the biscuit with a grateful smile. 'I'll have one more and shove off.'

Eventually, Mary arrived. She was sorry to be late. She had bumped into Oliver on his way to the South Mine. They had stopped to chat about his opal ring, for which he had left a deposit, and about his calling in to Harvey's to pay the final instalment.

Rosalind was leaving Stack & Tyndall's at the end of a trying Friday afternoon when she heard Gül's bell again.

She continued on down Oxide Street and then

stopped and checked a non-existent watch, and paralysed by her own recklessness, turned and trod in heavy steps along the pavement she had once tripped over, scraping her knee, when she was a girl.

There was a cardiac thump underfoot. Horses tethered beneath shop verandahs jerked back on taut reins. Rosalind was accustomed to muffled subterranean explosions, although since August these had become less frequent. New was the reverberation in her chest.

She saw the white cart trundling along Argent Street and walked towards it with a face that Gül immediately knew was for him.

The fracture in his glance came from what people like her had done to him, she told herself. He shook the reins, but she grabbed the harness and held it. She knew how to stop a cart.

His horse snorted like a flag unflapping. There was the smell of animal sweat.

She raised her eyes. 'I have something for you,' and dug into her pocket.

Curious, he looked down at what she had given him, coiled in his palm like a young tiger snake, before awkwardly stretching it out: a lace from one of William's boots.

Rosalind waited for Gül to thread it before she questioned him. And though he was not in the mood to talk, she did eventually get it out of Gül: what Oliver's officious uncle had said when he called at Lakovsky's ice-house in Blende Street.

This was the story Gül told.

Dowter interrupted Gül in the little front room, damping casks, and asked him what he was doing, and Gül said, 'Damping casks.' Dowter then said, 'You will get into trouble.' Gül said, 'How will I get into trouble? Mr Lakovsky makes the ice-cream in that room over there that has been made by the rule – as you know.' Dowter then stepped into the refrigeration room, but on this occasion not to check that the motor was functioning, or that the temperature was at 22 degrees below freezing point, or that none of the cans had their lid off, or that his instructions to Lakovsky as to the concrete floor had been carried out. The Sanitary Inspector seemed to be looking for something else.

Whatever Dowter hoped to find, it was not in the cans that he emptied with tremendous fastidiousness onto the floor and examined in messy succession.

Dowter was on the point of leaving when he saw a rolled-up object at a lean against the wall. He walked over and unravelled it with a kick. He bent down, a deceptively cheerful expression on his face, and plucked out, with no apparent effort, a length of reddish wool.

Looking at Gül, Rosalind remembered the rug she had sat on in the camel camp, its strange patterns and motifs, lozenges and zig-zags, woven in brown, crimson and indigo. With unusual clarity, she saw Gül laying out his mat in the refrigeration room, where no one would see him, to say his noon prayers. Later, some loose strands must have brushed off him when he was filling a can, and fallen in.

So my guess was right, she exclaimed within herself.

'And you haven't heard from him again?'

Gül shook his head, but he could not shake from his mind a very angry Meester Dowtah threatening him with a large fine.

Rosalind pieced it together; it was easy to piece together. There was only one reason why Clarence Dowter had taken no further action. He did not possess a sample of the contaminated ice-cream, as the Pure Food Act demanded. Rosalind had swallowed the only proof. And felt a tickle in her throat from the woollen ghost of it.

'He was angry because he realised he couldn't fine you.'

Rosalind was so absorbed by where her thoughts

were leading that she scarcely registered Gül saying he had to go – he had glimpsed the flustered shape of Mrs Lakovsky, his boss's wife, pushing a large perambulator across the street. Rosalind watched him kick the side of the cart, and was pleased when his boot stayed on.

The incident brought them together. Whenever Gül's horse and cart appeared, Rosalind felt an internal tugging combined with a surge of relief.

How often did they meet in the next five weeks? There were blanks which no one would be able to fill in. But it wasn't hard to bump into each other in Broken Hill.

It became harder to tear herself away. Rosalind's fear of being discovered in conversation with a 'Turkey lolly' was mingled with an unfamiliar feeling, a loosening of something inside her in which excitement and possibility were present too. His skin might be brown, and yet Gül had a heart not so different to hers, and a good heart, it seemed to Rosalind.

She would not have been able to talk in a coherent way about their relationship, if that is what it was. It was something private, mysterious, and she felt it spreading. She began to spend the money that she had been saving for her wedding dress on ice-creams.

People who observed Rosalind with Gül saw a young woman at the head of a queue of snottering children wiping their noses and bawling at her to get a move on. Sometimes she stood there with Lizzie, who from the start associated Gül with the sugary tastes that she liked so much. Over the past three years, it had become automatic at mealtimes for Rosalind to contract into a state of vigilance – to ensure that Lizzie didn't choke on her food. But ice-cream was safe, the way it slipped down your throat. Good for invalids, too, apparently.

Lizzie became her alibi.

By Christmas, there wasn't a single one of Lakovsky's flavours that Rosalind hadn't sampled, to say nothing of the sodas, milkshakes and Bijou syrups that were Lizzie's favourites.

Once, Rosalind caught Roy Sleath looking in her direction, his nose jutting out like his father's truncheon, and said, 'I have to go.'

Otherwise, only Mary Brodribb appeared to sense anything. 'How's your new boyfriend?'

'What are you talking about?'

'I saw you with him outside Harvey's.'

'Oh, Gül Mehmet you mean . . .' and said something about Lakovsky, the boss, needing extra milk in a hurry.

Mary did not believe her. 'Positive you're not keeping something back, Ros?'

'I most certainly am not!'

Mary glanced at Rosalind. She heard a lot of things in Harvey's. 'You know what everyone says? It gives you the fits, not to say what you feel.' The truth always came out in the end. When a woman had something on her mind, to stop her saying it was as foolish as trying to cover a shaft-head with a handkerchief.

But it was dangerous to tell Mary what was on her mind. Mary was jealous of her relationship with Oliver Goodmore, and Rosalind had a sharp hunch that Mary would be willing to trade in her friend for the fiancé, without really knowing or understanding that that's what she was doing.

Mary aside, no one came forward to say that Rosalind Filwell had developed an uncharacteristically sweet tooth all of a sudden, or that she and Gül seemed to be doing more talking than the act of buying an ice-cream required. At the intersection of Wolfram and Kaolin streets. Outside the Freiberg Arms Hotel, while he watered his horse. Coming out of Lakovsky's ice-house holding a churn. And on another occasion, going into Gilbert Bros., the saddlers.

Lakovsky's decision at the end of November to order his milk from Rosalind's father made it easier for their encounters to pass unnoticed. The stickiest beak in Broken Hill wouldn't have found reason to linger over the sight of Albert Filwell's daughter walking with a metal pail in each hand to the ice-cream maker's factory in Blende Street. And if the white cart with Lakovsky's name on it sometimes stopped in the street to give Rosalind a lift with the milk, this too was nothing remarkable.

After an initial wariness, Gül asked her questions, what she believed in, where she'd been, about her ashen-haired mother, who washed and darned for extra income. And about Lizzie, whose condition he appeared to understand. Rosalind's friends knew Lizzie as a peculiar girl with a big forehead that she compulsively rubbed, and who talked to herself as though permanently frightened by something inside her. In Gül's village near the Khyber Pass, he'd had an aunt like that, he said, with a lot of stones in her head.

Curiosity was strong in Rosalind. Gül seemed to have travelled the world. One afternoon, he produced from his waistcoat pocket a creased postcard of Hagia Sophia, and described with passion the vivid colours that the grainy black and white photograph failed to evoke. He put his hands on hers when she tried to return the postcard. 'No, keep it.' Their hands stayed together for a moment, one on top of the other.

The following afternoon, he quite badly ripped the back of his hand on a splinter while shifting the ice-cream chest to make space for one of her milk buckets. She produced her handkerchief and used it to wrap the torn skin. It gave her a small charge, dressing his cut, to have confirmed what she suspected all along. His blood was the same vermilion shade as the red that bloomed in her underwear, and which she was never able to anticipate in time.

She was envious of what he had seen. His visit to Istanbul, the sailing boats and minarets and tiles bluer than the sky. Is this what Miss Pollock dreamed about behind her sun-faded curtains on Oxide Street, and which accounted for her starved look? Broken Hill was resistant to comparisons. Milk, cakes, mining were what Rosalind could talk about. Gül represented life beyond the mullock. He was proof that Rakow Street was not the only street in the world.

The things he knew! He planted images in her mind. Suffocated by inevitability, she longed for what she was lacking. All she had was this flat landscape and this huge sky, black snakes, brown snakes, and the tan-coloured slag-heap with its blue and green stains on the rocks from the minerals that had been extracted. And Oliver Goodmore, of course.

She was reminded of Oliver every time the ground shook and the horses neighed. But she kept him out of their conversations.

What Rosalind learned from Gül was what he chose to reveal to a twenty-one-year-old girl who had been nice to him when no one else had. In time, others would take part in a frantic scramble to piece together Gül's history after treating it with disdain.

Back in January, she had asked her father, 'Where do you think *they* come from?' and nodded across the road at the team of camelmen who were noisily rescuing the Filwells' bungalow from the sand. Her father had been going on with thwarted pride about Rosalind's grandmother, a Doughty, who had come from a cottage in Farranavara in County Cork, bringing out with her to Australia the four-poster rosewood bed that he and her mother now slept in, and in which each of the three Filwell children had been conceived as well as born. Yet he never exhibited a smidgeon of interest in the background of anyone in Ghantown, their origins, or names. Turks, Hindus, Afghans, Indians – they were much of a colour. His eyes darted over to the pot-bellied foreman, whom she afterwards realised was Molla Abdullah, and he said simply, 'He looks like he comes from a good paddock.'

She could have written it on Gül's postcard, all that she knew about him. In her strong, small hand, as Miss Pollock had taught.

Gül was an Afridi from the Tirah Valley who had landed in Australia seventeen years before, in the dark hold of a ship chartered by an Afghan who had promised him £3 a month to look after camels. Gül's idea was to send money back to his family and at the end of a three-year contract go home. But there was not enough work as a cameleer, and he had found himself destitute. With no money for the return passage, he had raked stones for ballast, done a bit of bore-lining, and cut up sleepers for the railway extension at Wilcannia, before he drifted down to Broken Hill where he coaxed an Irish miner to teach him how to use a hammer and drill, wangling himself a position as an underground trucker for seven shillings and eight pence a day. He saved enough, he told her, to travel to Turkey, where he stayed for a time, but on his return to Broken Hill he found that the miners had been laid off after all contracts with the German smelters were cancelled – the Germans being the principal buyers of lead and zinc from Broken Hill. He went back to cameleering, walking strings out to the sheep stations with post and provisions, and returning with wool bales. But the war did not spare the camel trade either, and in early November he had bought an ice-cream cart off an Italian. His initial encounter with Rosalind in Argent Street took place after he had been hired to ride his cart around Broken Hill to hawk Leo Lakovsky's ice-creams. He admitted to her that it wasn't Lakovsky who had taught him his English, but a team of sandalwood cutters from Tarrawingee. He also said that he had not given up his intention of going back to settle in his native land.

Rosalind could not have said that she *knew* Gül. She never penetrated his mystery or understood him; they were different as two coloured threads crossing each other at right angles. He went into that box of people like Miss Pollock who had prised open her curiosity. But he had the effect of the cockatoos that screeched in the gums bordering the creek; he made the place less lonely by his presence.

For Gül, too, the chaos stopped when he saw her, his horror of what had been done to him faded, as did his fear and continual loneliness among infidels.

Who persuaded who? To some in town, Gül was the mastermind; to others, it was Molla Abdullah. Most likely, they evolved their plan together in the days after

Gül was ejected from the Trades Hall. It wouldn't have required much instigation. Gül, by then, had endured a bellyful of derision. And Molla Abdullah was going berserk anyway, having been fined a second time by Clarence Dowter.

According to who you listened to, the two men hadn't known each other long. Or else they had known each other many years. Not in dispute was that Molla Abdullah, following a fire at his home in Williams Street, was living in temporary accommodation in a ripple-iron shack right next to the hessian humpy that Gül had moved into when he returned from his latest travels.

Gül was friendly and open, more thoughtful. His neighbour was an old cameleer with a limp. Some years before, Molla Abdullah had got between a raging camel in *musth* and his cow, and the bull camel had torn a chunk from his right leg. Ever since, Molla Abdullah had walked in a doubled-up manner, like someone battling indigestion, or waiting for the next stone to land on his head.

Children go for you in a small town, where stone throwing too often is regarded as one of the joys of life. Different skin colour, strange clothes, not Anglo-Saxon – Molla Abdullah, a reserved, simple, childlike man, presented a target that was irresistible. Boys laughed when he shambled by and chased him down the street. He never retaliated, but he complained on more than one occasion to Sergeant Sleath, who each time promised to have a word with the rascals.

Molla Abdullah had other reasons to feel embittered. As well as acting as the imam at the camel camp, leading the group prayers on Friday and performing burials in the absence of a permanent religious leader, he served as the butcher of his community, killing their meat in the correct Muslim manner. The fact that he was not a member of the Butchers Employees' Union in the most unionist town in the country had brought him into confrontation with those who needed no excuse to treat a Pathan from India's north-west frontier as an enemy alien.

Since his arrival in Broken Hill eighteen years before, Molla Abdullah had slaughtered and prepared his meat in the North Camel Camp, out of sight of the town. He had received no reprimand from the council up until the moment, a year before, when Oliver's uncle became the local Sanitary Inspector.

Perhaps it was because Clarence Dowter was not qualified that he was overzealous. He had tried twice to get his inspection certificate, and failed. 'Why should the council carry Mr Dowter in its arms?' was the inflexible opinion of Alderman Turbill. But after

Turbill was dismissed and asked to hand over his keys, Mayor Brody had turned to Dowter, whom he had got to know when Dowter was in charge of the gang laying the Silverton-Broken Hill water-pipe.

In 1913, Dowter was appointed Acting Chief Sanitary Inspector. He might not have a certificate, but he had a bit of push behind him. Plus he was a union man. He wouldn't be another of 'those silvertails who gave no fair deal in the Sanitary Department'.

Dowter set to work, and no one enjoyed immunity from him. On discovering the state of the floors in the council toilets, he installed a penny-in-the-lock slot, and chastised the men and women in the council whose sense of cleanliness, he said, 'did not redound to their credit'.

Determined to prove himself in his war on scarlatina, diphtheria, pneumonia and typhoid, Dowter became a tyrant against all filth. To keep Broken Hill's premises in conformity with the requirements of the Pure Food Act, he fined a shopkeeper who sold butter which, in Dowter's opinion, was 'not fit for greasing boots'. He chased a man riding in a suspicious milk cart – 'the more he cried whoa! the faster he'd go,' reported the *Barrier Miner* – and when the cart toppled over, after striking a stone, stayed only long enough to collect eight samples. He prosecuted one woman for selling a verminous stretcher; another for tipping her soap suds into the lane.

As well, he hunted down anyone he suspected of contravening the Broken Hill Abattoirs, Markets, and Cattle Sale-yards Act.

During his first year in office, the uncertificated ex-pipe-layer issued summons to two butchers for transporting their meat in uncovered carts. He stopped one man in Slag Street who actually was riding on the meat, with flies following like seagulls. His dungarees were saturated in blood all the way to his ankles, and a leg of lamb was about to fall off. Dowter charged a third butcher for storing his mincemeat on a floor covered with a 'quantity of slimy stuff'; plus the owners of two piggeries for failing to keep their premises clean. But the person he monitored with the fiercest attention was Molla Abdullah, the Ghantown butcher.

Already, Dowter had found reason to caution Ghantown's residents, after discovering that they had dug an unauthorised grave in the town cemetery, in the small plot reserved for Muslims: all graves had to be dug by council gravediggers, Dowter was stern in reminding them – although it was permissible for Afghans to prepare the body and place it in a coffin, provided they left the screws undone.

Dowter found it offensive that local Afghans and Indians would not eat meat killed by people other than their own. Soon after his appointment, he had received a letter from the Ghantown community appealing 'in the name of religious liberty' for Molla Abdullah to be able to kill their meat at their camp and not in the abattoirs, where sheep and cattle were slaughtered alongside pigs ('one of the tenets of our faith is that the latter is a contamination'). The Abattoir Committee had turned down the request on Dowter's recommendation. 'There are people of fifty different religions who will want the same privileges.'

Molla Abdullah was not going to be made an exception.

Dowter prosecuted him for the first time that April, for slaughtering sheep at the North Camel Camp instead of at the municipal abattoirs. In court, the Ghantown butcher had read haltingly from a piece of paper: 'Me not guilty, not know break law, very sorry, not do again.'

Ordered to pay a fine of £1, or go to prison for seven days, Molla Abdullah had paid the fine. Dowter had not pressed for the heaviest penalty of £20.

A fortnight after he had walked into Stack & Tyndall's to question Rosalind about the purity of Gül Mehmet's ice-cream, the Sanitary Inspector visited

Ghantown again, and found four sheepskins strung out on the fence.

He cast his eyes about for Molla Abdullah and saw him crouched over a fire. Smoke gusted from a black pan where something was boiling.

At the sight of the Sanitary Inspector, Molla Abdullah forced a smile which revealed two brown teeth, and slowly got to his feet.

He stood staring at the ground, waiting.

In an unemotional tone, Dowter recited the regulation that each butcher's carcass slaughtered at the abattoirs must be branded with a distinctive brand in indelible red.

'There is no brand on these carcasses.'

Molla Abdullah looked up. The sun glinted on his scalp. 'No unstan, no unstan.'

'You said that last time. But not understanding is no defence.'

Molla Abdullah repeated himself.

To the Sanitary Inspector, the man's store of English was annoyingly small. Dowter thrust his right boot forward and with the toe began to scratch a circle in the earth.

In the adjacent humpy, a woman pulled open the door and looked out and then turned and whispered to someone inside.

Inquisitive faces appeared at window-frames to listen. Molla Abdullah's voice rose, imploring. The Sanitary Inspector said nothing. His foot went on circling. It might have been creating the world.

It was during their stand-off that Gül emerged from the humpy and walked over.

Dowter immediately recognised Gül from the ice-cream factory in Blende Street. When Gül offered to interpret, Dowter gave him a mistrustful and dismissive look. He hadn't forgotten the contaminating prayer rug. 'Don't think I haven't got my eye on you, too. But seeing as you're here, you can ask your mate if he killed his sheep in this yard.'

Gül turned to Molla Abdullah and the two men spoke animatedly. Yes, he had killed the sheep here. But the abattoirs had been on strike.

Dowter looked incuriously at Gül. The fact that the abattoirs may not have been *in use* did not mean that they were not *open* for use. It did not relieve a butcher of the necessity of complying with the Act. Nor did it justify a man killing surreptitiously and in an underhand way. 'What he's done is not legal. So he's going to be fined for doing it.'

Grabbing Gül's arm, Molla Abdullah wanted his position explained to Dowter. He swore by the beard of the Prophet and the bones of his seven ancestors that he sold only to his own people, and not under any circumstances to the general public.

'Is that right?' said Dowter meditatively. He reorganised more dust with the toe of his boot, as if he might find something buried there. 'Then maybe you can ask your mate here if he is a member of the Australasian Federated Butchers Employees' Union?'

This time, Molla Abdullah was fined £3 and ordered to pay the six shilling costs of court. The police magistrate gave him until the end of December to pay, or face imprisonment for one month.

A desert was closing around the old man. He heard his name in a denigrating tone being knocked about the courtroom, in a language he did not speak or write, and he wondered how his life could have ended up so soiled.

After leaving the courthouse in a rush, Molla Abdullah bashed his way up the street. A hard object struck him on the shoulder and he spun round, glaring. He grabbed the stone from the pavement and hurled it back at the goading group of boys and girls, causing one girl with sores on her face to yelp.

He lumbered on. His temples ached. Back in

Ghantown, he wallowed for the next two weeks in an apathy from which no one could stir him, save for Gül Mehmet.

Late on Christmas Eve, Gül returned to the camel camp and entered Molla Abdullah's shed, looking agitated. He produced a small fistful of hashish and they sat on the ground smoking it through a long-stemmed bamboo pipe, discussing grievances.

Gül was pugnacious after his eviction from the Trades Hall. He had maintained his composure until he stepped outside the building, but as he walked home with his two companions, he couldn't rid himself of the image of Rosalind Filwell, her look that went through and beyond him.

Yet she had done nothing to restrain Oliver Goodmore and his jeering mob.

His thoughts streamed out as he recalled Goodmore's face, and how Alf Fiddaman and Roy Sleath had shoved him towards the exit, calling him a mooching Turk. These white men and their families were honoured guests at the festivals in the camel camp. Why should Gül and his friends be denied entry to a dance in Broken Hill? Wasn't this Gül's town as much as it was Goodmore's? Didn't Gül Mehmet and Molla Abdullah have British passports too?

So they raked over old grouses. As the night wore

on, their sense of injustice magnified along with their impotence to redress it.

Molla Abdullah still felt utterly dejected by the fortnight-old court case. He had no means of paying the £3 fine by the end of December. The fire that had destroyed his uninsured two-roomed house in Williams Street, while he was boiling a pan of fat, had burned his possessions, including all the money he had. He had lost everything. And in less than a week, Dowter's strict application of a set of regulations that contravened his religious principles and made no sense to him threatened to take away his freedom.

Both of them should have returned home a long time ago, said Gül with a thoughtful sigh.

Molla Abdullah tugged at his beard and shook his head from side to side in anguish. Even if he could have afforded the passage, none of his family in India were alive. He had nothing to live for – and thanks to Dowter's unions, he wasn't even allowed to dig his own grave!

Ever since he had arrived in Australia, nearly two decades before, Molla Abdullah had been cooking his humiliation and shame, rendering it down, and now, sitting in this smoke-filled shed with Gül, it exploded into indignation.

The Turkish Sultan was right. Europeans like

Clarence Dowter were an offence to Islam – and Oliver Goodmore and his friends no better. They were cutters of the veins of life. They were unclean pigs.

Neither Gül nor Molla Abdullah needed reminding that Turkey was at war with Australia, and that the Sultan, only five weeks earlier, had appealed for a jihad against the Entente Powers, 'the mortal enemies of Islam', obliging all Muslims young and old, on foot or mounted, to support it. Had war broken out sooner when he was in Istanbul, Gül admitted, stretching out his long legs, he would have joined the Turkish army and fought.

Probably it was then that Gül made his bold proposal: they should answer the Sultan's call to arms, and seek a glorious death by attacking his enemies thousands of miles from home. Branded as Turks, what did they lose by behaving like Turks? Instead of living this persecuted existence in Broken Hill, wouldn't it be better to die with the guarantee of happiness in the next life – by killing as many Australians as they could? The Australians were doing all these terrible things to true believers, not only in Broken Hill, but in Egypt and no doubt imminently in Turkey. Why not go for them here, in Broken Hill, in the desert?

Molla Abdullah's eyes sparkled like flames spitting up from a heated pan, catching fire, running across the hessian. So did his house in Williams Street burn down.

But in the morning the heat and light had not diminished.

The decision made, Gül felt serene, weightless. The only person who had treated him well in the community which he now saw as his duty to destroy was Rosalind, and possibly her sister. But he no longer thought of them. He had crossed into an existence, parallel to the one in which he woke up next day and went about his business, that enveloped him in a rapturous calm.

Gül and Molla Abdullah never again smoked hashish, but over the next six days they had conversations. They discussed what form their crusade should take. They made a reconnaissance of the railway line – coming back from this, Molla Abdullah's camels had collided with Albert Filwell's milk buggy. And they fixed on a time and a day: the morning on which Molla Abdullah was to be arrested.

Date and location agreed, they acted swiftly. The butcher took charge of tailoring the Turkish uniforms in which they had vowed to fight; the ice-cream seller, because he spoke English, organised weapons and ammunition.

Gül required the rifles for hunting rabbits, he told

the publican in Slag Street who sold them to him. He said nothing to Frank Pincombe, at whose store Gül paid two shillings for eighty soft-nosed Snider cartridges, but Pincombe was more than pleased to get rid of such old stock. Across the street, Gül bought two extra-strong cartridge-belts, each three foot nine inches long and one and three quarter inches wide; and two pairs of leggings, which he picked up on New Year's Eve.

In the same hour of that same evening as Rosalind prepared the mutton and lettuce sandwiches in her mother's kitchen in Rakow Street, the two men sat in Gül's humpy and dyed a cotton tablecloth with sheep's blood. Onto this crimson background, Gül stitched a yellow crescent moon and a star to resemble the Ottoman flag. They folded it away in the ice-cream chest, along with the cartridge-belts, a Belgian navy revolver, a new butcher's sheath knife, and the two rifles: a Snider-Enfield for Molla Abdullah, which Gül had bought for £5; for himself, a Martini-Henry breech-loader with a long steel barrel.

As the sun fragmented behind the date palms, each wrote out a confession to tuck under their cummerbunds.

In his confession, written in a mixture of Urdu and Dari, Molla Abdullah explained that he bore no enmity against anyone except Clarence Dowter. 'One day the inspector accused me. On another I begged and prayed, but he would not listen to me. I was sitting brooding in anger. Just then the man Gül Mehmet came to me and we made our grievances known to each other. I rejoiced and gladly fell in with his plans and asked God that I might die an easy death for my faith. I have never worn a turban since the day some larrikins threw stones at me, and I did not like it. I wear the turban today.'

Owing to his grudge against the inspector, Molla Abdullah's intention was to kill Dowter first.

Gül wrote: 'I must kill your people and give my life for my faith by order of the Sultan because your people are fighting his country.' He thought to add that he had informed no one else of his intentions – he did not wish to implicate Rosalind Filwell.

That night, the two men walked back and forth three times through the doorway of the mosque and read from the Koran and said their prayers, in accordance with Molla Abdullah's instructions. The idea of his death did not frighten Gül, when he considered the glory which awaited and the luxuries bestowed on those who died in the struggle.

With their heads pointing north, they snatched a few hours' sleep, then rose early to perform a ritual shaving and cleansing. They washed their bodies thoroughly with water from a billy can, massaging hands, forearms and feet with perfumed oils and musk. After scissoring off his beard and razoring his chin, Molla Abdullah put on a collarless shirt trimmed with silk. He wore rings on his fingers and toes, kohl around his eyes, and on his bald head a small blue skullcap decorated with mirror fragments and embroidered with a frieze in the style favoured by the desert tribes around Kandahar. Last, they put on their red jackets, leggings and white silk turbans.

Shortly before 5 am, the two-man army of Allah climbed onto Gül's ice-cream cart and rode out of Ghantown behind his bay horse, down Rakow Street, following the railway line towards Silverton, to declare war on Australia.

Three

'Grab your seat for the joy ride!'

'Don't push!'

Above Rosalind, the smoke from the Y-class loco-motive hangs vertical and motionless in the air, like one of Oliver's pipe-cleaners.

Almost the last to board is Miss Pollock, who creates a flurry on the platform, in an orange dress down to her knees, high white boots, elaborately laced, and with scarlet and emerald ribbons twisted around her calves in tango style.

There's a three-note whistle. Jim Nankivell, the driver, leans out of the locomotive and waves. At 10 am, after various jolts, the longest and most crowded picnic train ever to depart Broken Hill pulls out of the station.

Beneath hats and parasols, hundreds of passengers settle down in the forty cleaned-out mining wagons, happily talking and waving; hampers and rugs tucked under the benches, and the swings that will be slung up over branches.

Rosalind looks around at her open ore-truck which once carried zinc and lead to Germany for bullets, and now carries Mrs Rasp, who is tinting her mouth with rhubarb lipstick.

Mrs Rasp has given up on Mrs Kneeshaw and is telling the Sanitary Inspector, between dabs, about her friend Alderman Turbill who shot himself in Adelaide two weeks ago – 'although he had no worries'. She licks her lips. These picnic outings make her talkative. She finds it a comfort to brood on her friends' failures and to feel exaggerated pangs of pity. 'He was found unconscious with a wound in his temple and holding a rusty gun in his right hand.'

Oliver is missing all this. Already, he has taken off his jacket and has gone to sit with Roy and Alf; they are bent over in a huddle, discussing the rugby. At least half the rugby union players of the state have joined the war, Oliver says severely. The local league will have to be reorganised for next season, and takes a long swig from Roy's waterbag.

The talk around Rosalind, who guards Oliver's place with her hamper to stop Mrs Rasp spreading herself, is of the foot-running at Silverton.

Mrs Kneeshaw from her corner catches Rosalind's eye. 'I think I know about Oliver' – his name becomes rather ugly in Mrs Kneeshaw's mouth; she suspects Oliver Goodmore of being one of those extremists who hurl stones and insults at departing recruits like Mrs Rasp's son Reginald – 'but will you be competing, too, today?'

It's something else that Rosalind has not decided. She moves the hamper a few inches to the right. The ore-truck has been hosed, but it still smells metallic.

She feels breathless, more than the overheated air warrants.

'I might do the single ladies' race.' And afterwards, while her mother and Lizzie visit a garden in Penrose Park, Oliver will walk her up the creek.

Mrs Kneeshaw is sympathetic. 'The extreme heat made it difficult for my daughter to reach the tape last year. And today might be hotter, I have the feeling.'

'Or,' pursues Rosalind, her breasts itching under her blouse, 'I could do the ladies' hammer and nail competition.'

Mrs Lakovsky utters bird-like coos at her newest baby, who smells of sour milk, while trying to stop her three-year-old Ivan from crawling under the bench. Small black flies go on sewing in the air. And Mrs Rasp continues to mourn her dead alderman. She looks very white inside her large dress and new straw bonnet. She could blot out the sun.

'They say the gun was faulty and may have misfired after he looked down the barrel and poked the live cartridge with a nail.'

'Something he sure was capable of,' remarks Mr Dowter, not hiding his venom. Alderman Turbill had been the one hotly opposed to the council carrying the uncertificated Dowter in its arms.

Mrs Kneeshaw is still looking at Rosalind. Thinking: she has a good figure and thick black hair; her face is rather plain. 'Are you happy at Stack & Tyndall's?'

'Oh, yes, Mrs Kneeshaw, I think so.'

'The Red Cross Society has a vacancy for a nurse,' and smiles. She has white teeth, some longer than others. 'Miss Pollock is convinced you would make a first-rate nurse, Rosalind. I am inclined to agree.'

'Me . . . a nurse?' Rosalind could not have felt more inarticulate if she had been asked to summarise Cornelius Hayball's Sunday sermon. Nothing has happened to her, and so she does not know anything. Oliver has his machines and his toolbox. How can she hope to repair anyone?

She looks down at her palms. 'I'm not certain I would be so good at *that*.'

'Well, if you change your mind,' says Mrs Kneeshaw, and leans forward. She wants to reach out. She has watched Rosalind with Lizzie. With Oliver as well. 'You know, Rosalind, you must always feel able to speak with me – if there is something you want to say.'

Suddenly, there is something Rosalind would very much like to say, but Oliver is wedging himself back in beside her.

The mullock lies in sunlight behind them, leeched of its shadow and power to intimidate. Oliver in his hat instead lours over her.

Out of habit, he starts packing tobacco into the bowl of his pipe. But it's too hot to smoke – even Clarence Dowter's cigarette has been returned with a snap into its silver case.

Oliver sits back, Mrs Kneeshaw too.

Over the low rim of the truck, the morning is a tangle of fences and roofs. The train passes along the houses, past the gardens, smelling a little of manure, slowing down at the Rakow Street crossing.

In the yard, the cows and heifers are lapping at the water trough. Their shadows stretch in puddles of black.

'That's your room, isn't it?' says Oliver, pointing with his pipe stem at the window, wanting to draw her in.

Her eyes linger on the small hard round shape in his

shirt pocket, on the hairs in his nostril, on the mouth-piece of his cherry-wood pipe. Once, toying with it, she had sucked and tasted the bitterest thing, a globule of gungy tar. *That* had made her scream.

'Yes.' She twists her lips; she has not stopped condemning him, the dirty fingernails of her future husband.

Oliver, on the other hand, is radiant. An hour ago, he was buying fruit for the picnic when Alf Fiddaman told him he had a house to rent in Mercury Street. The couple who lived there were relocating to Hobart with their two small children.

'Would you come and see it with me, Rosalind?'

'If you would like.' The words, positive but neutrally spoken, hide her dismay.

'What about tomorrow?' He can't look at her enough, although his uncritical gaze does not suit his face, which the sun is painting red. He moves closer. 'Alf says it's perfect for a young family . . .' And their shadows join on the floor of the truck, to melt into a rearing, tussling creature.

She looks as though about to turn herself into something sweating.

'I think . . .' The words are too big to get out of her mouth. She senses Mrs Kneeshaw watching as she answers at the second attempt.

'Maybe tomorrow,' and adjusts her pink hat.

There is a veil between them, but he doesn't seem to notice.

The train creaks and bumps forward again.

She shuts her eyes to stop him seeing. The sound of the Bosphorus is inside her ear, and white triangular sails are tacking across her eyelids. She looks at herself on the edge of the Red Sea, dressing wounds.

When she opens her eyes again, Clarence Dowter is removing his jacket. He takes out a watch and notes the time, then stares glassily across at her as if he can read what she is all about in a notice under her chin. She remembers the carpet that she denied swallowing, and smiles.

'Emmy didn't want me to come, but I have yet to miss an Oddfellows' picnic.'

Her father's familiar laugh gives Rosalind an excuse to glance away. Up against the end of the truck, backs to the engine, her family are seated in a row.

Rosalind had not wished to sit with them. She had boarded the train without resolving her argument with her mother about Oliver. But now she doesn't want it left untreated.

Arm in the fresh sling which she had fitted on him that morning, her father is chatting with a small, cheerful-looking man wearing a large bow tie.

Rosalind leans forward, and waves to catch her mother's attention; it concerns her that she might still be feeling unhappy. But her mother is engrossed in Lizzie, who is rubbing the fuzz off the peach that Oliver gave her.

Her sister was the sensitive one, her mother believed. Who would sit up in bed, shrieking.

But for Rosalind that was always William.

If Lizzie was all sky, she and William had been earth.

She remembers after her brother's accident when her father took her into the mine. Hurtling down. Water dripping from a dark rock face, and the terrible heat. The cage stopped. There were lots of lights. And at the end of a tunnel, an office with a man in shirt-sleeves standing over a huge ledger, like the ticket office in the railway station, and men signing in. 'This is William Filwell's sister,' her father said. 'She wanted to see where he worked.'

For the first time, the darkness feels thicker where she is. Her brother is behind her and she cannot hear him. As if a bell jar has descended and silenced her.

She's had her tongue cut out too long, she tells herself. In the passive feminine way which, once silenced, becomes poisonous. And yet here she is, about to choose a man, a good enough man, but one who wants to participate in the cutting of her tongue.

The train builds up steam near the Picton sale-yard, then slows abruptly as it approaches the cutting.

Clarence Dowter volunteers the reason – the sticky-beak has heard it from the driver himself: Jim, he says in his dry voice, has been instructed to take it easy here, since the previous week the express was held up after the wind blew a foot of sand over the rails.

Rosalind twists around and looks down over the side of the truck, but really to escape Mr Dowter and his small grey eyes.

She gazes at the humps of sand beside the tracks, at the intricate lace-like paths of the sandhill beetles foraging for food, and thinks of the wedding dress worn by her cousin Louise, living in a tiny room in Beryl Street while her husband is fighting in Egypt.

Rosalind has exhausted on Gül's ice-cream the money she had saved up for her dress. And suddenly feels tedious, she who has received a postcard from an Afghan; her parents and Oliver never knew about that.

The designs tremble and fade. She is left with Oliver's hard arm pressing into her thigh. She sees the veins snaking under the backs of his hands and remembers Gül's hand, and how she had wrapped it with her handkerchief – actually, her grandmother's handkerchief – that he has yet to return.

The palms of her hands are sweating. She feels it under her skin. The ingrowing wick of her unlit, and perhaps unignitable, passion for Oliver. Lost in the shadow of his brim, he is not the answer to any mystery.

Her thoughts are running over each other up the bank, and sliding back. The train picks up speed. Soon it will burst out into an ocean of baked red earth, of opalised shells and fish and long-extinct sea-monsters, but already she is retreating into her own tableland of five-inch rainfall, denuded of mulga scrub for miles around, all removed for fuel; a bald and empty region like his sandy-haired head would become.

By the time the train draws parallel with the lime kiln, Rosalind has decided what she will say to Oliver Goodmore.

The cutting is the perfect spot from which to mount a surprise attack, and will be cited as proof of Gül's military experience. Because of the lime kiln, none of the passengers have a full view of the line. The Ottoman flag comes into sight separately to each wagon only as the train sweeps around the curve.

Lawrence Freer, the fireman, is standing out on the footplate when he notices a red cloth fluttering above a white cart. His first thought: someone's exploding defective ammunition. But he dismisses it. No one would be venturing out with a powder magazine on New Year's Day.

The cart is parked near to the tracks, on the other side of the trench with the water-pipe. The train steams closer. Freer reads the words italicised on the side, and relaxes.

'A bit late for the ice-creams to be going out to Silverton,' he observes to the driver.

Jim Nankivell smiles. 'I suppose some poor old beggar's hoping to make a bit for himself.'

They chug past, and Nankivell sees what looks like an insignia on the red cloth. A breeze has sprung up, ruffling it.

At that moment, a pair of white shapes bob up from the trench – dark faces, the tips of rifles – and he hears two gunshots. One bullet hits the sand, spraying dust against the engine. The second bullet strikes the brake-van, embedding itself in the woodwork.

Ralph Axtell is sitting in the brake-van with the Mayor and the secretary of the Manchester Order of Oddfellows.

'What's that?' enquires the Mayor.

'It's probably the Germans,' shouts Axtell, who has postponed his return to Melbourne until after the picnic.

The Germans! In Broken Hill! Everyone laughs. They think it's a stone pinging against the side.

The two turbaned men continue to fire at the train, ducking down into the trench to reload, or to take cover in case anyone shoots back. But no one is shooting back. No one has any idea what is happening.

'Hurrah!' contributes someone, responding to another shot.

Jabez Herring, Clarence Dowter's deputy in the Sanitary Department, scans the horizon through his gold-rimmed spectacles, and sees nothing: 'They're only firing blanks,' he reassures his wife.

Then: two puffs of red dust.

Miss Pollock in her orange dress feels impelled to lean over the side and call out at the empty landscape in her teacher's voice: 'Stop fooling around, or someone will get hurt!'

A pair of girls in Mary Brodribb's truck yell 'Happy New Year!' at the spectacle of two dark men in such candid white turbans and red jackets.

Mary smiles, but her eyes are unhappy, seized by the thought that this may be a surprise which Oliver has organised for Rosalind, and the shots are being fired in celebration of their engagement.

Next to Rosalind, Oliver jerks up his head.

'What the hell?' rising to his feet. He sees a cow on the right-hand side and wonders if some idiot is trying to shoot it. Just then, he spots Tom Blows ripping along beside the pipe-track, his round face protected by a leather visor. He thinks, *It's Tom's motorbike back-firing!* and takes off his hat, waving it in the air, at the same time delighted to notice, strapped between the handlebars like a crib tin, the small case containing Tom's camera equipment. *Even if I haven't managed to fix the problem, he should be able to make it out to Silverton.* Tom is photographing the running races at the picnic ground. In return for Oliver repairing his motorbike, he has offered to take a joint portrait of Oliver with Rosalind afterwards.

Clarence Dowter leaps up next. He registers two men lying on the embankment above the trench which contains what the Sanitary Inspector has come increasingly to regard as his life's work: the reticulation pipe that he laid ten years ago to carry 80,000 gallons of water per hour from the creek at Umberumberka to Broken Hill. He assumes something must be wrong with the water-pipe – a leak perhaps – and these men are attending to it.

Lizzie is clinging to the side and waving the peach that she has started to eat. She is pointing it out – her beloved ice-cream cart. She wants the train to stop.

Rosalind, emerging from indifference, now stands up and squeezes in between Oliver and his uncle. Confusing matters, the *ka-bang ka-bang* of the motorbike. But she is puzzled by the white cart. It hasn't travelled far since she saw it last, five hours ago, outside her window in Rakow Street, and is turned about as though coming back to town. Has a wheel broken? Gül should be in Silverton by now. She feels a stab that he will miss out on so many customers.

It's then that Rosalind sees the yellow crescent like a banana, and a star.

She looks around. At the horse on its own under a tree. Less than thirty yards from the train, the Ghantown butcher lying on his belly. And crouching on the embankment another ten yards away – Gül.

Their turbans are frost-white, like ice-cream almost.

The train is carrying her towards them.

Suddenly, Oliver tenses. 'Get down, Rosalind!' and grabs her. But his hand on her arm does not comfort.

'I am not going to get down.'

Uncoercible, she raises her right palm to attract Gül's attention.

Behind her, Mrs Lakovsky is thrusting her children to the floor. 'Ivan!' she is shouting. 'Ivan!'

*

Earlier that morning, shortly after 9 am, Gül spreads out two horse blankets over the pipe in the trench. He sits there with Molla Abdullah, waiting more than an hour. When they hear the rails tremble, they jump to their feet. Gül shoots at the driver and misses. Molla Abdullah shoots at the fireman and misses.

Stooping to reload, Gül again asks Allah to accept his sacrifice. Then he levels his barrel at the line of passengers who have stood up.

In white shirts and hats, peering over the side, in the roasting sun – all those unbelievers, waiting to be picked off.

Gül fires, reloads, fires once more, startling a wood swallow from the mulga. He springs out of the trench to join Molla Abdullah on the embankment.

Legs apart, Molla Abdullah wriggles forward. He has only ever used a gun to shoot sick animals and is not accustomed to the kick. Still, what easy targets – these goggling women wearing ridiculous clothing. Like a row of rabbits in their soft cotton dresses, or a goat he has to kill for fresh meat when on a month-long hawking trip to Corona.

'*Rabbana inna aamanna, fa ighfir lanaa thunubanaa wa qina athaab el naar . . .*'

Molla Abdullah completes the *istighfar dua* prayer asking for forgiveness, and fires.

In the second truck, Jabez Herring drops like a coat from a hanger. His spectacles fly off, clattering to the floor. Above him, one of his wife's brothers grabs Mrs Herring by the floppy sunhat which she has fastened under her chin, and tugs her down.

Molla Abdullah reloads. Another truck rattles slowly by.

He raises the rifle to his shoulder, and looks down the barrel at a man with an arm in a white sling – all at once recognising the rider of the milk buggy which had crashed into his camels. It wasn't Molla Abdullah's fault that the dairyman never reined in his horse. And this was the man whose house he had dug out of the sand!

The butcher is about to pull the trigger on Albert Filwell when his attention is diverted by Clarence Dowter squinting in his direction, as though he is beginning to interrogate him again. Molla Abdullah's eyes are black opals above his newly naked chin. If he could pick off the Sanitary Inspector, who has now removed his hat . . .

Abruptly, he shifts the barleycorn foresight from Rosalind's father until it hovers on Dowter's face.

At that instant, Gül notices Oliver Goodmore. He tries to quell his rage, asking Allah to give him patience, and takes aim.

Two loud reports, one after the other.

Pinioned between Oliver and his uncle, Rosalind feels a blow, followed by heat.

Lizzie lets go of her peach. It rolls under a bench, picking up grit and droppings. She jumps down to retrieve it, inspecting the moist flesh embedded with flecks of quartz and earth, and starts to shake.

Oliver, though, realises they are being fired at. He turns to Rosalind, but she has slumped forward.

He puts his arm out to support her, and as he does so blood streams down his wrist. He catches Rosalind by the shoulder and lowers her to the floor of the truck. Limp in his arms, she has never seemed so relaxed, so intimate.

She looks up at him in a perplexed way.

He stares back at her, his mouth wide open. Part of her forehead is missing.

'Rosalind . . .'

'But I . . .' Her voice sounds as if it doesn't come from within her, but from another place.

The train pulls up a few yards further on while driver and fireman debate what to do. Jim Nankivell can see people in the cutting ahead. Are there more attackers waiting along the line?

Molla Abdullah kneels and fires. He appears to be aiming at Jack Crossing, an assistant guard in the last wagon, who jumps down and runs off.

Gül has stopped shooting. He stands on the railway track, staring at the ever smaller train.

He knows that the bullets intended for Oliver Goodmore and Clarence Dowter have missed their target. The way he cried out when he saw who was hit made Molla Abdullah think it was Gül who had been shot.

Gül had noticed Rosalind too late. He can still see her waving at him.

In the fierce light, the confusion of the ore-truck is laid bare. Children blink alarmed eyes at the panic taking place above them. Legs bumpy with varicose veins kick out from under skirts. The floor is a mess, suddenly, of dropped hats and parasols. Everyone is shouting.

Mrs Rasp has subsided on the bench in a cloud of white, from which red is oozing, spreading through the white picnic dress to her waist. Under her cream bonnet, she appears to have on a balaclava. The lower part of her face is knitted with blood from her masculine jaw, where a flying fragment of bone from Rosalind's skull has hit it. Blood drips from her mouth onto Rosalind's wicker hamper, and splashes to the floor.

Her moans mingle with those of Mrs Lakovsky, who has a big jagged hole in her left shoulder.

Amid the kicking and screaming and the scrummage to get the hell down, only Clarence Dowter stands unscathed above the commotion. He remains at the side of the truck, staring out, with the serious, strained eyes of someone having their hair cut. Upright and remote, as if perceiving in a mirror for the first time the contours of his own skull, he seems afraid to unlock his gaze from the trench carrying his waterpipe, and from which he appears to be under attack.

Behind the Sanitary Inspector's rigid back, Mrs Kneeshaw summons every ounce to put into practice her recent Red Cross training. She bends down beside Mrs Rasp, assessing her injury, and gently wipes her jaw with a handkerchief. Passing swiftly on, she twists her veil into a sling to support Mrs Lakovsky's shoulder.

But it's Rosalind Filwell who most needs help.

Her father is uselessly trying to shade her face. Her mother holds both of Rosalind's hands, stroking and squeezing them.

When the train rocks to a halt at Tramway Dam, Clarence Dowter turns around.

Some force has dragged Lizzie's eyes inwards. She is juddering and choking and rubbing her head vigorously, as if in the grip of a fit.

Clarence Dowter looks down at a semi-naked Mrs Kneeshaw. And a sight that remains with him until his death in Kogarah seven years later, of his nephew Oliver cradling Rosalind's unrepairable head.

Mrs Kneeshaw has finished tearing up her petticoat into bandages. She ignores Lizzie's shrieks and convulsions, and, nudging Oliver aside, starts to bind Rosalind's wound. The back and top of Rosalind's head is practically blown away, and her brain exposed.

Rosalind imagines that it's the Afghan who tenderly wraps the strip of white cotton around her temple.

She is conscious of a glaring light. The sun is a miner's torch bearing down on her.

'Goo . . .'

'I'm right here. I'm with you.' Oliver's shadow falls like lead across her blouse.

'I don't know why . . . I . . .'

She is bleeding from the mouth, but she wants to say something.

*

While Mrs Kneeshaw bandages Rosalind's forehead as best she can, Jack Crossing, the assistant guard, has hared down the track to the reservoir at Tramway Dam, where he finds a hand-cranked telephone in the pump shed. He turns the handle and waits for an answer.

Two more shots ring out from opposite the cemetery.

The receiver is picked up by the station master in Broken Hill.

Crossing gasps that the Manchester Unity picnic train is under attack from soldiers flying the Turkish flag and that several passengers are killed or injured, and armed assistance is needed.

The message is relayed to Sergeant Sleath at the police station.

At 10.45 am, the Reverend Cornelius Hayball is driving Mrs Stack down Argent Street in his Ford runabout, having picked her up outside her store. They are on their way to Silverton when the policeman flags down the car.

'I need you to take these four men to the Freiberg Arms Hotel.'

The men climb in. Sergeant Sleath dives into a second car. The two vehicles, loaded with a total of ten armed policemen, accelerate off in convoy towards

West Broken Hill, leaving Mrs Stack on the pavement.

With fresh rumours reaching shocked ears every minute, a spontaneous posse of about fifty men is raised from a crowd that has gathered in front of the police station. It comprises members of the Barrier Boys' Brigade Rifle Club, but soon embraces any able-bodied volunteer who owns a gun and would like to have a lash.

The local military commander is contacted. Major Sholto Sinclair-Stanbrook of the newly formed 82nd Infantry Battalion is leaving for the Jockey Club to watch the horse races, when his adjutant runs out to say that he is required on the telephone.

Appointed to his command because he 'looked the part', Major Sinclair-Stanbrook consents to Sergeant Sleath's request to deploy his men. Since it is New Year's Day and most of the battalion are off duty, the order is issued for any soldier who hears about it to muster in ten minutes at the Barrier Boys' Brigade Hall in Oxide Street.

All thoughts of the hurdle race suspended, Major Sinclair-Stanbrook voices the confusion that many feel: Are they dealing with lunatics, or with highly trained troops? If the latter, where have the enemy sprung from – the mining town is 300 miles at least from the coast. And if the Germans or their Turkish allies have in fact reached as far inland as Broken Hill, in what numbers are they here?

Oliver never sees the shot that kills Tom Blows as he roars, exhaust pipe popping, towards the ice-cream cart. His motorbike slithers along the ground, spewing photographic equipment, and comes to a halt beside the trench.

The train has disappeared through the cutting when the two men stand up and walk over to where Blows lies jack-knifed in the sand. Molla Abdullah has shot him between the shoulders.

Molla Abdullah kicks for signs of life. Gül stoops to pick up a lens that has spilled from the burst camera case. He peers through it – he looks like a camel who has strayed, with his inflamed rims – and tosses it aside. Molla Abdullah says that armed men will soon be chasing them, they had better leave this place. Gül nods in an absent way. This is wrong. He keeps seeing the white palm of her hand, waving.

Gül goes over to the ice-cream cart and tugs down the flag; and then they abandon their position above the water-pipe, their horse and cart, and trudge back on foot towards Broken Hill.

They thread their way across a flat expanse of

stony, treeless desert dotted with wind-twisted, blackened vegetation and the skulls of gourds and paddy melon, resembling two shepherds from the Holy Land in their khaki coats and turbans. Molla Abdullah has his rifle slung across his back, Gül carries his in his hand, and the red flag. It trails on the ground behind him, blurring into the red earth.

Quite soon they come to the isolated houses on the western fringe of town.

Old Phil Deebles, a retired fettler, is first to see them. Unaware of what has occurred, he calls out in a jocular voice over the wicket fence that he has all but finished painting. 'You won't get much shooting round here,' waving his brush.

Gül looks at him and walks on.

Terence Riley, a seventy-year-old tinsmith with a spade-sized black beard, is standing in his doorway when they pass. 'You'd better not do any shooting here,' he growls, 'there are children around.'

Without warning, both men raise their rifles. The tinsmith slams the door, but they fire through it, shooting him in the abdomen. Clutching his stomach, he staggers out of the back of his house and clambers down the granite slope to the Freiberg Arms Hotel.

They trudge on, skirting the West Camel Camp north of Kaolin Street, where several Indian and

Afghan camel drivers live. Badsha Khan is milking a goat in front of his shack. Gül fires at him and shouts, 'Don't follow me, or I'll shoot you,' and fires again.

Near the Freiberg Arms Hotel, Sergeant Sleath notices two figures ambling along the ridge, and drives up, intending to ask if they have seen the enemy. The car is bouncing towards them when the men kneel and shoot. Constable Torpy steps out to return fire and is hit in the groin, twice. He lies sprawled in the shade of the Ford's swung-open door, cursing.

Gül and Molla Abdullah climb to the top of the hill, and look for shelter behind an outcrop of white quartz boulders. Moments later, something pokes up from between the rocks. It's their flag, knotted to the end of a dead branch, a bright red diagonal against the blue sky.

By the time the relief train arrives at the reservoir with fifteen armed men on board, Rosalind is dying.

Mrs Kneeshaw has had to take tremendous care in bandaging her head, as there's nothing left of the exterior of the skull to hold the brains in position. She uses Rosalind's hat to swat away the flies that keep congregating.

'... I can't ... I thought ... no ...' Rosalind could have been sleep-talking.

Her eyes flutter. She can hear her sister screaming.

Lizzie's voice thins out – a long way above now. Because Rosalind is plunging, somersaulting into the earth. As when she went down with her father in a cage to see where her brother had died, and she sank in a clatter, the wind fanning her face, into a vast chamber of gleaming pin-points, of lead sulphides twinkling in the darkness, or stars.

Oliver is leaning over, looking down. He is close to her face. She can smell his breath, a faint perfume of peaches.

'Gool ...'

'Ros ...'

'... so sorry.'

A vagueness enters her eye and then her shattered head falls sideways.

Gül and Molla Abdullah have chosen a good position to defend. The police are exposed and disorganised, dotted out in the open on the barren slopes below.

Sergeant Sleath's first attempt to dislodge the two men from their hilltop is met with defiant shouts of *'Allahu Akbar!'* and a brisk burst of gunfire. One shot chips a piece off the boulder behind which Sergeant Sleath skips to take cover. Another loose shot kills Ern Pilkinghorne, chopping wood in his yard; deaf, the impervious veteran of Pongola Bosch has heard nothing of the battle taking place opposite.

In town, dazed shock has given way to fear and then to fury. Tom Blows's body has been retrieved from the cutting, his face still wrapped in his visor and with his sun-reddened ears poking above the strap. Also, the corpse of Jabez Herring; his coppery hair is matted with blood and a piece of gut protrudes from his back.

Argent Street is full of men charging about with rifles.

'The bloody bastards!'

'We're not safe while they're alive!' another shouts.

The correspondent of the *Barrier Miner* notes that in their desperate determination to leave no work for the hangman, the mob have developed little mood for compromise.

By 11.30 am, reinforcements are streaming towards the Freiberg Arms Hotel to assist Sergeant Sleath. They arrive by car, on foot, in a slop cart, in any vehicle they can obtain. All eager to repel an enemy that no one expected.

The white rocks are on a rise less than 300 yards

from the hotel. In a wide circle around the summit crouch fourteen policemen; forty-three volunteers from the Rifle Club; thirty-three passengers from the picnic train – some still dressed in white linen suits – including Roy Sleath and Alf Fiddaman, who have each run home and fetched their father's rifle; plus fifty-three members of the 82nd Infantry Battalion under the command of Major Sinclair-Stanbrook.

The battle lasts two hours and fifty minutes. Still, it seems to take an awfully long time. How two men, both not very effective shots, are able to keep at bay a heavily armed party ultimately numbering several hundred is not a question that anyone feels much motivated to pursue. It is, though, generally agreed that each and every member of the attacking force behaves splendidly.

Major Sinclair-Stanbrook is confident that he can position the Turks by the black smoke from their guns. He knows the battles of the Peninsular War by heart. Buçaco, Vimeiro. This was Salamanca. He is Wellesley. After assessing the situation, he stands up – broad shoulders, aquiline nose, a scar on his cheek from a clash with a nail – and in a firm, imposing voice calls on them to surrender. 'Come out with your hands up. We've got you surrounded.'

Two bullets enter the earth at his feet. Ducking, he hears a hoarse shout: 'Australians – burn in hell!'

A pair of miners have brought along sticks of dynamite to chuck as hand grenades, but more shots drive them back.

For a moment, silence. The sun burns directly overhead as if gummed to the sky. Heat waves dance off the slopes. There is the firework smell of gunpowder.

Then voices are heard from behind the rocks, chanting. The two men have no water. Their croaked prayers resound over the battlefield.

'. . . *la illah illaa huwa wahdahu la sharika lah, lahu el mulk wa lahu al hamd wa huwa ala kulli shai'n qadir . . .*'

Major Sinclair-Stanbrook, peeping with caution above a wool bale, spots through his field glasses a dark object flitting between the white rocks. He orders his men to fire at it.

The barrage does not let up for five minutes.

Shots echo back and forth. Chips of granite fly. The red cloth crumples to the ground, the branch snapped by a bullet.

Molla Abdullah hurls himself after it, shouting '. . . *la ilaha illa Allah . . .*' He staggers down a little from the rocks on the other side, and stands still, clasping his rifle, staring with abject eyes at his flag.

Major Sinclair-Stanbrook is momentarily nonplussed, but Sergeant Sleath bellows, 'Fire! Fire!'

They all shoot at the same time.

Molla Abdullah flings up his arms and collapses, not moving.

Sergeant Sleath has run out of ammunition. He scrambles back behind the Freiberg Arms Hotel to obtain a fresh supply.

When Gül sees Molla Abdullah fall, he says another prayer.

'*Allahumma inni astaghfiruka li thanbi wa as'aluka rahmatuka ya Allah!*'

The skin below his eyes has a sunken look. He is still not afraid. Only for Rosalind, who might have died an infidel.

He pushes a cartridge from his bandolier and reloads. Twenty-two cartridges left. He wipes his brow with the end of his turban, lifts his rifle.

Gül keeps firing for about an hour and then his shots become less frequent, less threatening. He is evidently badly wounded.

Just before 1 pm, he is observed rising to his feet. Short of breath, exhausted, he holds his arms out with difficulty. They are not carrying any gun. But in one hand he clutches what appears to be a white handkerchief.

Someone shoots at him and misses. He flattens himself against one of the rocks, glances around, and withdraws behind it.

'Reckon he's trying to surrender?' Sergeant Sleath asks.

'No,' says Major Sinclair-Stanbrook. The muscles show on his jaw.

When no more shots are heard, Major Sinclair-Stanbrook directs twelve men to advance in an open line. They wheel in from the left, climbing the hill in a series of nervous rushes, twenty steps at a time, rifles ready to butt.

Several bullets are fired in quick succession as they reach the top, before Sergeant Sleath calls out, 'Stop!'

A mixed mob of police, military and civilians then surges up the slope – to find the two turbaned men lying motionless on the ground a few yards apart. They trot forward like wild cattle to examine the bodies.

Molla Abdullah, still holding onto his rifle, has been shot between the eyebrows. Gül has sixteen bullets in his body – in his chest, neck, right forearm, and left thigh. The fingers of his left hand are lacerated, and his right hand is wounded, wrapped around by a dirty handkerchief with blood on it.

Sergeant Sleath notices a movement. Gül has

opened his eyes and is trying to speak. A water bottle is put to his lips. He is barely alive, but he smiles as though he might have recognised the person who has appeared out of the heat to nurse him, and even has expected her.

Four

Weeks later, in the Saxon town of Freiberg, the manager of the Berzelius smelting works opened the *Leipziger Volkszeitung* and read the following:

> *We are pleased to report the success of our arms at Broken Hill, a seaport town on the west coast of Australia. A party of troops fired on Australian troops being transported to the front by rail. The enemy lost 40 killed and 70 injured. The total loss of Turks was two dead. The capture of Broken Hill leads the way to Canberra, the strongly fortified capital of Australia.*

Not long afterwards, a force of 20,000 Anzacs lands on the Gallipoli peninsula in Turkey. The Third Australian Brigade consists largely of miners from

Broken Hill. One of the bullets from the ore he dug up goes into the head of Reginald Rasp.

In Broken Hill, on the opposite side of the world, the confused happenings of that Friday morning take the rest of the summer to unpick. A narrative of sorts emerges in the *Barrier Miner*, which publishes interviews with survivors. Each survivor tells a slightly different story. Not only that, but they seem to reweave it with every recital, so that strand by strand the previous pattern of events unravels to be reworked into a fresh version, and the ritual repeated, pushing the experience past living memory and out of language.

Rosalind's undertaker delivered the coffin with her body in it to the Filwells' bungalow in Rakow Street, where members of the Manchester Order of Oddfellows, in regalia, had gathered with members of the Master Dairymen and Milk Vendors' Association, together with teachers from Rosalind's school, and the staff of Stack & Tyndall's. A sizeable crowd followed her hearse to the cemetery, to the sound of the Salvation Army band playing 'Nearer My God to Thee'. At Rosalind's graveside, the mourners lined up behind her sister and parents, and joined the Reverend Cornelius Hayball in singing at the top of their voices 'Sweet By and By' and 'Safe in the Arms of Jesus'.

Hayball gave a brief address, a tall, thin man with spectacles that sat uneasily on his nose. 'No one can know when the golden thread of life might snap for us. No one can understand why this tragedy has happened.' He paused, quite out of breath. Privately, he felt overwhelmed by what he had seen at the hospital on that outrageously hot afternoon. Naked bodies on tables. Rosalind and Gül lying side by side, their knees and hands almost touching. And the perspiring figure of Dr Large on the telephone, trying to get through to Leo Lakovsky's refrigeration room in Blende Street, to order extra ice before the bodies started to decompose, so that witnesses might identify them and the coroner perform autopsies. Hayball could only tell the congregation that God understood and knew all.

Sergeant Sleath had contacted Rosalind's undertaker to bury the 'Turks' as well, but he refused. The policeman next commissioned a municipal gravedigger to prepare two graves in the Muslim section of the Broken Hill cemetery. He began digging these on Saturday evening in a corner up against the fence, but being given no further instructions, beyond that the work should commence at once, he dug the graves at right angles to the fence, with no particular attention to where they pointed.

That night, a crowd roamed the western hills after torching the German Club in Delamore Street, and noticed a man digging. They protested: if these graves were for the Turks, they would tear up their bodies from the earth. The digger at once threw down his spade. He did not know who the graves were for, but if they were for 'those damned Turks', cowardly slaughterers of defenceless women and children, he was not going to complete the job.

The two half-completed graves in the cemetery, pointing not north to south, but north-west to south-east, remained empty until the next dust storm.

Over the years, the sand has filled them in. Still today, no one knows where the bodies of Gül Mehmet and Molla Abdullah lie buried. As if this strange and tragic event had occurred and then been blown away by the desert winds, until there's nothing much left or remembered.

Author's Note

Although inspired by events that took place in Broken Hill on New Year's Day 1915, this is a work of fiction; the characters are, in large part, creatures of a novelist's imagination. Gül Mehmet and Molla Abdullah did exist, but little is known of their background, and what information has passed down to us remains uncertain and contradictory. I am grateful to Murray Bail for introducing me to their story and for taking me to Broken Hill; to Brian Tonkin, Archives Officer in the Broken Hill Council; to staff of the Broken Hill Library and Railway Museum; and to Felix Ogdon. I would also like to pay tribute to *Tin Mosques & Ghantowns: A History of Afghan Cameldrivers in Australia*, by Christine Stevens (Oxford University Press: Melbourne, 1989). The quote from the *Leipziger Volkszeitung* is taken from Steve Packer's article 'The odd angry shot', *Sydney Morning Herald*, 3 January 1998.

UP THE GANGWAY AND OVER THE WAVES

Sarah E. Francis

To my shipmate Barbara with love and good wishes for calm seas and interesting landfalls.

Sarah E. Francis

ARTHUR H. STOCKWELL LTD
Torrs Park, Ilfracombe, Devon, EX34 8BA
Established 1898
www.ahstockwell.co.uk

British Library Cataloguing-in-Publication Data.
A catalogue record for this book is available
from the British Library.

Chapter Four: SS *Canberra*, reproduced with kind permission of ©
Dashers under the terms of the GNU Free Documentation Licence.

Chapter Five: Fairmount Banff Springs Hotel, reproduced with kind
permission of © Hedwig Storch under the terms of the GNU Free
Documentation Licence.
Glacier Bay, reproduced with kind permission of © Janquen under the
terms of the GNU Free Documentation Licence.

For my dear friend Beryl Zillah Wilson
of Brantford, Ontario, Canada.

ISBN 978-0-7223-4401-9
Printed in Great Britain by
Arthur H. Stockwell Ltd
Torrs Park   Ilfracombe
Devon EX34 8BA

CONTENTS

UP THE GANGWAY AND OVER THE WAVES

HOW IT WAS

"And if you had been on as many troopships as I have, you wouldn't want to go on a cruise either."

Can it be more than thirty years since Himself was pontificating in this manner? "I remember in the early years of the war we embarked from Glasgow on the *Orduna*. She had been condemned in 1936. Down on the orlop deck when the lights went on we heard crunching noises and found we were inches deep in cockroaches. There were so many rats on that ship that the Captain offered a shilling a tail. By the time we reached Cape Town they were all gone."

From time to time I uttered encouraging words like "Yes" and "No" and "Fancy", and busied myself with my own thoughts until he returned from Hong Kong a second time.

As I mused, I recalled that our holidays had been of a hit-and-miss variety – some successful, some not so good. The time we toured Scotland, visiting "every sanguinary battlefield in the country", according to Himself, was not one of the better sorties.

Stratford and the Cotswolds did not raise his spirits either. We got tickets to see Laurence Olivier hanging upside down by his feet (I forget why) in *Coriolanus* at the Royal Shakespeare Theatre. In those days we could not afford to stay in reasonable hotels, so the mattresses were hard and the food was indifferent.

In the early sixties the currency allowance was restricted to £25 per person when we went to Paris. Later, Himself complained to anyone who would listen that I made him walk round the sights of the city all day on a continental breakfast and a tube of wine gums. This seemed logical if we were to make the money last and have a decent evening meal.

One day we stopped outside the English Church and debated whether to go in and look at the architecture. The Bishop came out and, discovering that we were English, he asked us to be witnesses to a wedding. The bride was a model, beautifully dressed, and the groom was in a morning suit. They had both worked in Paris and had decided to be married there before going home to have family celebrations.

We were in what Himself termed 'scruff order': I was in an elderly Marks & Spencer's dress and he looked a bit unironed as usual. He was best man and I gave the bride away. Later we celebrated with champagne at a place on the Champs-Élysées. They asked what we were doing for the rest of the day. We told them that we were going on a trip down the sewers from the Madeleine to the Place de la Concorde. Together they said, "Can we come with you? Please wait for us until we get changed." Thus began a friendship that lasted over fifty years.

I will gloss over going on a small ship (only six passengers) with a cargo labelled 'Pickled pelts, Malmo'. I worried lest they were cats' pelts. The vessel tossed about in the North Sea; the china was flung on the floor, but my Scottish and Yorkshire blood reminded me that we were paying £5 per day (all in) for this trip, so I stuck it out. Two students were sharing a cabin and the one who turned up for meals told us that his companion was on his knees praying to die. We left the ship at Copenhagen and were picked up a few days later.

In between times we travelled to and fro across the Atlantic by air to visit cousins and friends in Canada. Once, in the good old days, we travelled first class for an extra £20 each. What a bargain – hot towels, marvellous food and Royal Doulton china!

Our family and friends in Ontario were kind enough to ensure that we were taken to all the tourist sights – Niagara Falls, Toronto, and down over the border to Buffalo to visit more family. We loved the relaxed lifestyle – so different from our stressed post-war existence in Britain. In Florida we went to Cape Kennedy and Disneyland and found the life even more relaxing.

Watching the pelicans diving into the sea at Daytona Beach was fascinating. Not so cheerful was the news that we could not get a flight home from Miami for three weeks. Instead we flew to Washington and gave a taxi driver (a huge Negro with a gorgeous smile) the rest of our dollars to take us on a tour of the city (the White House, Arlington Cemetery, etc.) before leaving us at Dulles Airport to go back to London.

By the time Himself had finished some of his wartime reminiscences I felt that we needed to broaden our holiday experiences.

It took quite a while for him to be persuaded, but eventually we boarded a cruise ship and travelled in great comfort with not a cockroach or a rat in sight.

CHAPTER ONE

UP THE GANGWAY

Our first cruise was an occasion for much angst on my part. Himself, having booked the passages on P&O's *Sea Princess* and having organised the taxi and traveller's cheques, absolved himself from further involvement. Neither of us can remember taking out what is now obligatory travel insurance. I expect we must have done so as we have always been insured for every calamity apart from the plague.

Meanwhile, I was much exercised about what to take, what clothes I would need, what to tip and numerous other problems. In those days we did not know many people who went on cruises. Two very good friends from Yorkshire – Doris and Bill – had been on the *Uganda*, famous for its educational cruises. They had enjoyed the experience so much that I have always felt it was their enthusiasm rather than my insistence that persuaded Himself to agree to go.

An elderly friend, who was rather wealthy and had been on several cruises, had some advice: "Take plenty of evening dresses, dear. You will need a different one each night. Casual wear on the first and last nights means not too casual, just your smartest frocks. Never mind the list of people to be tipped. I hand a £5 note to the cabin steward and the dining-room steward and say, 'Look after me well and you will get some more.' It establishes one as a person of substance."

All this made me worry more than ever. I had a couple of evening dresses and set about borrowing more garments from friends. I bought a long black velvet skirt to team up with some tops and never dreamed I would be wearing it more than thirty years later.

Himself had an old evening suit which he wore for the occasional formal dinner and for concerts with his choir in 'Dear Albert's Hall'. A friend assured me that the suit might one day come back into fashion. His evening shoes, black patent leather, had once belonged to his Aunt Mabel's father (she died at well over eighty) and Himself refused to be parted from them because they were so comfortable.

For some reason or other our itinerary was altered due to the arrival at Heathrow of the Pope. We were lodged in a hotel near the airport ready for an early flight. The entrance was draped with hangings made from knotted wool. The decor was of purple, red, yellow and orange geometric shapes on walls and carpets. We spent an uneasy night and were happy to leave to catch a plane at 6.30 a.m.

How civilised air travel was in those days! We were given glasses of champagne as soon as we were airborne and were offered continental or cooked breakfast. The pilot told us about various landmarks as we passed over them. As we flew into Athens Airport I remember thinking that even Socrates had never seen Piraeus from this view.

Down at the quayside we joined a long queue and it began to rain. The *Sea Princess* looked sleek, white and beautiful, but our admiration was somewhat dampened by the weather and the long queue. Himself (in those days often on a short fuse) spotted the Captain and dashed off to accost him. The latter blamed the Greek immigration officials for being so slow. Himself suggested that the Captain should go on board and hurry them up a bit. This he did, and in a short time the queue moved quite rapidly. Himself must be the only person to complain to a captain of a ship before he had even set foot on board.

Our cabin was pleasant and spacious. There were two single beds on either side of the porthole (no balconies in those days) with four wardrobes, of which I filled three. The sitting area had two armchairs, a fitted desk-cum-dressing table, a phone and a radio (the radio purveyed Muzak and the BBC Overseas Service). The bathroom was well equipped with bath and shower. Fresh water and a basket of fruit were welcome additions. There was also a passenger list, but it was of little use to us as we knew nobody on board.

A leaflet entitled 'Who and What to Tip' listed cabin steward, table waiter, wine waiter, head waiter, assistant head waiter and section waiter. Other recipients (if applicable) were night steward, nursery steward, lift and bell boys, and bathroom(?) steward. I thought about my friend and her £5 notes and felt she had the right approach.

On the first morning our steward told us that an old gentleman in the next cabin had died in the night. It appeared there was a procedure for this eventuality; a lady steward and officials were with the widow full-time.

"Perhaps she will choose a burial at sea," said the steward. "It is a beautiful service." Later he informed us that she had declined this offer and her family were flying to Haifa to take him home.

On the first formal evening everyone, especially the ladies, was dressed up to the nines. It was the Captain's Cocktail Party and long queues of people formed to have their photographs taken with him. Later came the Captain's Dinner, and afterwards we had a choice of activities – a classical concert, theatre, cinema, cabaret, gambling or dancing. We went to the concert.

Our first port of call was Haifa. I thought Himself would have wanted to take a tour of the Holy Land. He had been among the very last troops, Royal Marine commandos, to leave Palestine when the UN Protectorate ended. They had provided a guard of honour for the high commissioner, who left with them on the last ship.

Contrary to my expectations he had no inclination to go

10

ashore. "You know I don't like being on a coach." Not even Jerusalem could tempt him. "We had enough trouble there and we used to escort VIPs from Jerusalem to Haifa."

I could see he was in a time warp so I did not press the matter. I intended to see as much as possible.

Armed Israeli soldiers came aboard when we docked. Some came into the dining room for breakfast, pistols very much in evidence. They stationed themselves at the bottom of the gangway and checked all movements on and off the ship. I boarded one of the coaches and we set off for Jericho. Himself told me later that after half an hour the passengers on board heard the sound of distant gunfire. We did not know it at the time, but the Israelis were moving towards Lebanon.

Our guide on the coach was called Israel; he was very knowledgeable, but he hardly stopped talking for hours. The scenery looked very biblical with olive and fig trees, orange groves, and sheep and goats being driven along by shepherd boys. We passed King Ahab's palace and Naboth's Vineyard as we sped on to Jericho. The ancient ruins were very impressive and the walls, or what remained of them, seemed too massive to have fallen so amazingly as recounted in the Bible. The city was green and fertile and there were soldiers everywhere.

We drove along the West Bank of the Jordan and through the desert to Qumran, where the Essenes had lived. Here we saw the remains of their civilisation and the caves where the Dead Sea Scrolls were found. As we gazed across towards Dead Sea, Israeli jets screamed across the skyline. There were settlements on either side of the Jordan river and I was surprised it was so narrow – hardly wider than a stream. Israel, our guide, blamed the Jordanians for taking all the water, and I expect they blamed the Israelis. We went along the Dust Road, which the Israelis raked every night and inspected every morning for footprints.

We returned to the Jerusalem road and went through the wilderness of Judaea with the mountains of Gilboa on one side and those of Judaea on the other. It was very bleak and barren. No wonder John the Baptist was so strange after living out there

11

for years! We passed many vineyards watered by a complicated irrigation system. The land on the West Bank was farmed by young men who were also soldiers. There were several kibbutzim – not primitive places, as I had imagined, but flourishing communities with substantial houses and well-farmed land. As we approached Jerusalem the sun shone on the buildings and the Dome and it really seemed to be 'Jerusalem the Golden' as depicted in the hymn. We passed through Bethany and were shown what is said to be the house of Mary, Martha and Lazarus. We drove round the city and up to the Mount of Olives, then down and had lunch at the King David Hotel, a magnificent building which replaced the one that had been blown up, full of British troops, by terrorists in the 1940s. The meal was excellent.

Later, we went on foot along the Via Dolorosa, stopping at each of the Stations of the Cross. It wound through the souk, which was lined with stalls and shops, but the guide would not let us stop, presumably because they were owned by Arabs.

The Wailing Wall, where men and women were separated, was fascinating. We women of the group had to cover our shoulders as well as our heads with heavy shawls; nobody who was wearing shorts or 'unseemly dress' was allowed to approach. The Church of the Holy Sepulchre was interesting, but I had strong doubts about the authenticity of the tomb of Christ. What about the Garden of Gethsemane?

To add a modern touch we were taken to the University of Jerusalem and the parliament buildings where the Knesset sits. Then we set off for Bethlehem, which was not on our itinerary, but Reuben, the driver, said it was only a few miles away so we went anyhow. It was very commercialised with souvenir shops everywhere, even in Manger Square. The Church of the Nativity, on the supposed site of the stable and the manger, was huge. It was used and cared for by various groups. Under one floor a fantastic Roman mosaic floor had been excavated. I think it was part of an older church founded by the mother of Emperor Constantine, she being an early Christian. Then we set off on the long road back to Haifa.

Limassol was our next port of call. Although Himself had been stationed in Cyprus for a short time the island held no fond memories for him. We took a taxi into the town and I was impressed by the colourful houses, the flowers and trees, but after a leisurely stroll round he hailed another taxi to take us back to the ship. All day on board there were numerous activities: bridge, chess, backgammon and craftwork among others. Mostly I enjoyed relaxing and reading during the day or going to the lectures about the ports of call or on subjects of maritime interest.

We docked at Izmir and I spent part of the morning browsing among the shops at the quayside. I was tempted by a lovely opal ring, but as I had not enough money with me to pay for it I had to go back to the ship and find Himself, who was on the sun deck. Protesting (as was his wont at being disturbed) we returned to the shop and he bought the ring. Later I went by coach to Ephesus, where St John is said to have written his Gospel after the death of Christ. Mary, the mother of Jesus, is also said to have lived there.

The ruins at Ephesus were huge and impressive, especially the remains of the ancient library. The place had such an atmosphere. I felt transported back through the centuries as I wandered around. Coming back to the present day, I decided I needed a lavatory, which turned out to be a hole in the ground with water running through. I had heard of 'squatting pits', but it was the first time I had encountered one. No doubt there are ugly Portaloos in situ these days.

On the leisurely days spent at sea I had many chats with other passengers. Many had been on several cruises and I realised we were real novices. Quite a few had been displaced from the *Canberra* or *Uganda* and the comments ranged from 'the dear old *Canberra*' to 'a floating Butlins with queues for everything'. Of the *Uganda* there were good reports except that it was 'a bit spartan' compared with the *Sea Princess*. All of them did a lot of grumbling about having to pay for the tours. Judging by the ones I had taken, I thought they were very good value and pinpointed the main places of interest in a few hours.

One afternoon at tea I sat with four Cockneys – two couples –

who had been on many cruises in many ships. They thought the *Sea Princess* was quite good, but not as luxurious as the *QE2*.

"You must go on *QE2*, ducks," they said.

'Chance would be a fine thing!' I thought to myself.

Overheard conversations were often more amusing than the face-to-face ones. Towards the end of the voyage I was sitting on deck reading when two ladies seated themselves nearby.

After some desultory talk the elder one said, "I cannot help wondering what your mother will say when you tell her that you have become engaged to a man you met on board only a fortnight ago."

The younger one replied, "I expect she will say, 'Has he any money?'"

I kept my eyes on my book and managed not to laugh.

The menus were spectacular, each one a work of art. Flora, fauna, ships and cities were depicted on the covers. The food was good, but not always as good as stated. One night at dinner I had Christmas pudding (in spite of the temperature outside), which was excellent. On another occasion we had grouse, which was so tough that Himself sent it back to the galley. This caused some consternation and the head waiter and maître d' rushed to offer alternatives and apologies. Thereafter they came to enquire if all was well at each meal.

Cadiz Bay was huge. I kept thinking of the lines from the poem 'Home Thoughts from Abroad':

Nobly, nobly Cape St Vincent to the North-west died away;
Sunset ran, one glorious blood-red, reeking into Cadiz Bay.

From the quayside we set off to travel the 100 kilometres to Seville, passing fields of sunflowers, palm trees, jacarandas, bougainvilleas and glorious hibiscus flowers on the way. It was very hot – the temperature was ninety-two degrees when we arrived in Seville and 104 degrees when we left. We visited the cathedral, large and ornate, mainly rebuilt in the early eighteenth century after being partially destroyed by the English pirates. We saw the tomb of Christopher Columbus and visited the palaces of the old kings and emperors. Due to the intense heat, I failed to absorb a lot of the historical details. As we wandered around the Santa Cruz area I envied the occupants with their gated gardens and lush green courtyards. All the shops were shut for siesta, so we were all very, very thirsty. No bottled water in those days!

The Bay of Biscay was calm when we crossed it, but the rain was coming down in stair rods. Himself sorted out the gratuities into envelopes ready to hand over later in the evening. He ignored the list, but tipped well above the recommended rate for good service in the cabin and dining room.

As I packed I mused on the cruise. It seemed to have gone well with very few complaints from Himself. Perhaps that was because we each did our own thing. I went on tours and he stayed on board. Could that be the pattern for the future?

It was a beautiful day as we sailed up Southampton Water. Eventually we disembarked, paid our dues at the customs (my opal ring) and set off for home.

Later I asked Himself, "Did you enjoy it?" to which he replied, "It was all right" – high praise indeed from him. As for me, I could hardly wait for next year's brochures to drop through the letter box.

CHAPTER TWO

OVER THE WAVES

I am always hesitant about using the word 'we' as Himself is inclined to ask, "Do you mean the royal 'we'?" Albeit, as we became more experienced cruisers we concentrated on the itinerary and ports of call. This had the advantage of offering opportunities to visit places we might not otherwise have made the effort to reach. In addition there were some places we were glad we had not gone to for a week or more.

Hence we found ourselves on our way to the Baltic and what was then called Leningrad, and we were back on the ship of our first cruise – the *Sea Princess*.

Before we embarked Himself had said, "I hope we don't get that idle cabin steward we had the last time we were on the ship."

We did get him and he was no better, often leaving the cabin untouched until after midday. Himself remonstrated with him and was told he had too many cabins to do and "Anyway, we are allowed until 2 p.m. to finish our work." Himself, usually the most generous of men, decided to adjust his tip accordingly, downwards.

On the first night we had a spot of bother in the dining room. As usual we had asked for, and got, a table for two, second sitting. We saw that the carpet under our table was covered with crumbs and bits of food. Himself asked the waiter to clear up the mess, and he replied that it wasn't his job. We refused to sit down until the area was cleared. The head waiter and maître d' materialised and the waiter cleaned up the carpet while the two of them offered their apologies. For a couple of days the waiter was very sullen, but gradually he came round and was quite pleasant. Perhaps he thought his tip was at risk if his service was poor.

Neither we nor any of them realised that in a few short years most of the service staff would be replaced by smiling, eager Indians, who looked upon the jobs as careers. Nothing was ever too much trouble for them. Many rose to be head waiters and maître d's, while some in the engineering department became officers.

Some of the ports of call were familiar to us, but there was always something new to see. In Oslo we wandered through the park to the old castle, Akershus. It was here that the traitor Quisling was shot after the war. In the harbour we watched young sailors climbing the rigging of a three-masted training ship.

After lunch I went on the *Kon-Tiki* tour. We stopped at Frogner Park to see the spectacular groups of modern sculptures in granite, iron and bronze. In the distance we saw the famous Holmenkollen Ski Jump. In the Viking Ship Museum there were three ships over 1,000 years old and a large collection of well-preserved implements. The *Kon-Tiki*, built of balsa wood, on which Thor Heyerdahl and his companions had sailed 4,300 miles in 1947 across the Pacific from Peru to Polynesia, looked very, very fragile. Next door to it was the papyrus boat, *Ra II*, in which he crossed the Atlantic in 1976. While the rest of the party were wandering about, I went across the square to see the *Fram*, Amundsen's ship. It looked huge compared with the others.

The weather was beautiful when we arrived at Copenhagen and the harbour was dotted with little white sailing boats. We ambled around the city and then went along to renew our acquaintance with the Little Mermaid. The following day I went

17

to lectures on Leningrad and Helsinki, our next two ports of call. Our passports had to be handed in for perusal by Russian officials, who must have come aboard in Copenhagen.

Himself had intended to go on the tour of Leningrad, but he was struck down by a bad tummy upset – Montezuma's revenge. He blamed the curry at lunch, but he had to cancel his ticket. We docked in Leningrad at what seemed to be a dilapidated and somewhat isolated quay. As soon as the gangway went down Russian soldiers stationed themselves at the bottom of it and stayed there all day. Other soldiers were scattered about the area and the dockers were quickly dismissed when their work was done. The place seemed a bit eerie with only a few soldiers in sight. No passengers were allowed ashore except those going on Intourist tours. We went through a large immigration shed and each of us had to pass through a booth. This had a mirror overhead and was well lighted, but a soldier standing at the back was in deep shadow. We surrendered our passports and in return received a brown visitor's card. Then we were led to the Intourist coaches.

Our coach was clean and comfortable with air conditioning and our guide spoke excellent English. First of all we visited the Rostrum and saw the huge columns beside the River Neva. Across in the distance was the golden spire of the cathedral of St Peter and St Paul, which was a museum like many of the churches. Leningrad (now St Petersburg) is known as the Venice of the North as there are so many canals and bridges in the city.

We stopped in St Isaac's Square to visit the cathedral and I asked the guide for directions to a lavatory. She said we had permission to use the ones at the Astoria Hotel – 'the best hotel in Leningrad'. Here, we were told, they had a letter from Hitler instructing them to have a suite ready for him when the city fell. It may have been the best hotel, but the loos were filthy and smelly, and there was no paper, soap or towels. Perhaps they were the ones reserved for the workers. We had been warned about the Russian loos, that they were notorious and one needed wellington boots to approach them.

18

Back in the coach we returned to the river and saw the fortress, which used to house prisoners, tsarist and others. The forbidding stone entrance was known as the Gates of Death. It reminded me of Traitor's Gate at the Tower of London.

The more we saw of Leningrad, the more fascinating it appeared. We stopped at the Field of Mars, a cemetery-cum-memorial where revolutionaries were buried under the flower beds. Somewhere along the way was a beautiful statue of Peter the Great, inscribed 'From a Grateful Russia'. Apparently Lenin, at an early stage in the Revolution, ordered that all statues, buildings and monuments must be preserved 'for the people' because they had been built 'by the people'. Thus many tsarist treasures were saved for posterity.

We went to a new modern hotel for lunch. Here the loos were clean, but again there was no paper or soap and a hot-air machine for drying hands did not work. The meal was interesting, but the service was abysmal. For starters we had bits of fish and meat alongside an orange blob which was definitely not caviar. This dish was accompanied by a bowl of tomatoes and black and white bread. The black bread was very good and I exchanged my white piece with my neighbour for her black one. The soup was full of vegetables and pieces of leathery meat which could not be cut even with a knife. I declined the main course – more leathery meat, rice, greasy potatoes and a mysterious vegetable. Pudding was hard meringue and runny ice cream, and the coffee was black and bitter. Throughout the meal our ears were assaulted by a very loud balalaika band and a singer.

In the afternoon we visited the Winter Palace, now the Hermitage Museum. It was built by Elizabeth, daughter of Peter the Great, but she died before it was completed. There were five buildings housing the treasures, but we saw only a fraction of them. We traversed rooms full of paintings; Renoir, Gauguin, Matisse, Monet and Picasso were all represented as well as Rembrandt and Canaletto. A Goya had been donated quite recently by a wealthy American oilman.

The rooms of the tsars were stunning; I have never seen

anything so magnificent. The walls were decorated with pure gold leaf. There were tables and furnishings of malachite, jasper and lapis lazuli and enormous chandeliers. The opulence was overwhelming. We were told that the rooms had been restored after the Siege of Leningrad and the pure gold work and crystal chandeliers were exact reproductions of the original settings. We had walked about three miles in the Hermitage, and our guide said if someone spent two minutes looking at each exhibit it would take ten years to get round the place.

As we left there were queues of Russians waiting to get in. We had been given priority because of being with Intourist. I asked what the huge square in front of the Hermitage was used for and I was told, "It is for manifestations of the people." I interpreted this as meaning military parades.

The next stop was the Intourist shop, where dollars and pounds were the only acceptable currencies. The store was a long, oblong building and, unlike Western stores, the departments did not connect. It was necessary to come out of one department, perhaps selling food and drink, and walk down the street to another department, selling toys and souvenirs. Change was given in the form of chewing gum or matches to make it up to the nearest pound. Everything was expensive, but the Americans among us were spending liberally, never mind the Cold War.

On our return to the docks we passed through the booth again and received our passports before boarding the ship. Himself said that at lunchtime the Captain brought in a party of Russian military for a meal and they tucked in like trenchermen. Having sampled the food ashore, I did not blame them. As we pulled away from the quayside the soldiers dispersed and the area looked bleak and deserted as the ship left Leningrad behind.

When we docked at Helsinki there was a large sign saying, 'Welcome to sunny Helsinki'. As we disembarked, each passenger was given a red rose by a beaming young girl – quite a contrast to our reception at the last port of call. Himself stayed on board while I took a tour of the city, which looked clean and pleasant. The sun shone and it was very warm, but we saw the icebreakers which were laid up for the winter. Apparently many houses have triple glazing and heating costs are high. In Senate Square there are examples of Russian architecture from the eighteenth and nineteenth centuries. This area is often used for filming when a Russian background is required. We saw the Helsinki Olympic Stadium and the statue of Paavo Nurmi, the Flying Finn. In a beautiful park was a stainless-steel monument to Sibelius.

At Stockholm the weather was poor and it rained for the first time on the cruise. I went on a tour of the harbour by launch and visited the City Hall and Wasa Ship Museum, but did not feel motivated to explore later in the day.

Our last port of call was Aarhus in Denmark, where a band of about fifty young women with a majorette played jolly tunes to welcome us.

We returned home again, tired but with many lasting memories. Our good friends Doris and Bill had stayed in our cottage to look after our two white cats – Castor and Pollux. If they had not looked after them, year after year, we would not have been able to go away so often. Pollux lived to be twenty-one years old. As we could never have put them in a cattery, we were fortunate to have such good 'cat sitters'.

"Ah well! Tomorrow to fresh woods and pastures new, as Milton said," I chirped.

Himself harrumphed and went on tackling the accumulation of post that awaited our return.

CHAPTER THREE

MOROCCO

As I headed down the gangway at Casablanca, Himself, who was watching from the promenade deck called out, "See if you can find a sheik who will swap me two camels for you."

A woman in front of me turned abruptly and shouted, "Cheeky devil!" while a man behind me said, "I should ask for a flock of sheep as well."

Why do men indulge in such schoolboy humour?

We had boarded the cruise ship, the *Pacific Princess*, at Tilbury, which was a grotty port in those days. There was a dark, cramped reception area and one small counter selling coffee and sandwiches. On the ship, changes had already begun to take place and we found that all the waiters, the head waiter (now called the table captain) and the maître d' were Italians. Dinner on the first night was a shambles as it was open seating with everyone able to sit anywhere. We prefer to have the same table for two for each meal and, after Himself had made his wishes quite clear to the maître d', we got it.

Among the 680 passengers there were numerous Americans, as well as Dutch, Spaniards, Mexicans and several Middle Eastern families, and for the first day we wondered if we were the only English people on the ship. Lisbon, Santa Cruz, Madeira and Gibraltar were all on the itinerary, but Morocco was the highlight with Casablanca and Marrakesh as the destinations. We boarded the coach for the three-and-a-half-hour journey to Marrakesh and drove off into Casablanca. With its huge skyscrapers and modern buildings it looked more like Miami than an African city. Our guide pointed out the luxury Hotel Excelsior and the place where Rick's Bar was supposed to be in the film *Casablanca*. In another large hotel was a Bogart Bar with stills from the film. Yet we all knew it was not shot in Africa at all. It was a case of looking at the 'place where the Woozle wasn't'.

We travelled across the desert on a very reasonable road which for many miles ran parallel to a railway and electricity pylons. These were all a legacy of years of French and Spanish occupation. There were dromedaries by the wayside and poor overloaded donkeys and mules, either pulling heavy carts or carrying overweight men. More donkeys were looking for food in fields of stone that could not really be defined as fields. From time to time we passed villages which had developed around oases. There were date palms with bunches of green dates hanging from them and prickly pears growing on stunted bushes.

After nearly two hours of travelling on a single-track highway we stopped in a village for what the Americans call a 'comfort stop'. Some people went into the building to buy bottled drinks. Others searched for a loo. As soon as we had descended from the coach we were surrounded by Arab children calling, "Dollars, dollars." They all knew that word. They were even begging outside the loos, which were very primitive. Two boys, aged about nine years, stood at the entrance with hands outstretched, saying, "Money, money, dollars, dollars." None of the children would be photographed except in exchange for money. When I did get a shot of two men on donkeys across the road they waved sticks and shouted at me.

On the coach we travelled for another hour or more until we saw in the distance the High Atlas Mountains, a fine background for the lush and green Marrakesh and its environs. We alighted in the Jemaa el Fna square, a vast area full of stalls, fire-eaters, snake charmers, soothsayers and Muslim preachers. A local guide was waiting to conduct us round the city. From the start we were surrounded by Arab children and adults selling belts, toys, knives and caftans or just begging. This was the pattern of our tour for the whole day.

We saw the wonderful Koutoubia Minaret, built in the twelfth century by the Almohads. Each face of the minaret reflected a different image of the gates of Heaven. We followed the guide to a carpet factory. Here, children and young girls were weaving the carpets. We were given mint tea while we gazed upon beautiful examples of their labour. An American lady bought four carpets and arranged for them to be sent to her home.

Off we went behind the guide to the souk and came eventually to an hotel where we were to have lunch. There was no doubt this place was different from any Western hotel. The walls were decorated with brilliantly coloured tiles about halfway up, and the rest was in carved wood. Geometric shapes were used in both cases as we were told that humans and animals are not allowed to be represented in Islamic art. In the main room where we ate, there were huge tiled columns holding up arches and a carved ceiling.

We sat on cushions and the food was placed in the centre of a low table. About eight of us sat around each one. Everybody had to dip into the same dish; but, as a concession, we were given plates and spoons, which we had to use for every course. We started with a salad of tomatoes and some unidentifiable greenery. I passed on this, thinking the offerings might not have been washed. Then came chicken legs cooked in a spicy sauce. The remains on the plates were scraped back into the central dish. Couscous lamb in sauce on a bed of rice was the next course. We finished with pieces of melon and a bottle of orange juice. All through the meal there was a cacophony of sound from musicians while stout young girls sang and performed belly dances. They were clothed in garments that covered them from head to toe – only their eyes and hands were visible. By the end of the meal the room was stiflingly hot. I went outside with some of the ladies to find a loo. It must have been a unisex one because we had to wait in a queue while an Arab man was performing his ablutions, splashing water over his head and face before turning towards Mecca to pray. No wonder there is such a shortage of water in these countries.

While we were making our way to the Bahia Palace, one of our entourage of Arab boys thrust a parcel of belts at me with one hand and slipped his other one under the flap of my handbag. I yelled, "NO!" and jerked the bag away in time. Nothing was taken, but I clung to it firmly from then on. An American man walking alongside managed to stop an Arab child taking dollars from his shirt pocket, and another caught a child of no more than six years with his hand in his back pocket.

The Bahia Palace, also known as the Palace of Mohammed V was full of beautiful tiled mosaics and little gardens and courtyards. It was cool and shady – a welcome change from the scorching heat. There was a large garden with two rooms on either side where the wives used to adjourn in the evenings, awaiting a visit from the King. From the palace we walked through the heat to the shops. This journey was hazardous as we had to cross two roads. I have never seen so many scooters and motorbikes in any city. The riders roared among the people and donkey carts in a frightening manner.

The souk was a maze of shops and stalls, colourful, smelly and slightly menacing. The guide went far too quickly through the narrow streets and our group became spread out and even more of a prey to the street urchins. We were led into a couple of shops to inspect the wares – jewellery, carpets, brasses and silver goods. Then he set off again without warning. I managed to join the tail end of the line. We learned later that a woman and her daughter had been left behind in a shop and had to pay $20 to a local to be taken back to the square and the café where some of the passengers had stayed behind. As we went through the souk, I glimpsed thin little cats and kittens and a few puppies for sale. Someone pushed past me carrying half a dozen headless chickens dripping with blood. There were men with bells on their heads, arms and legs, banging and ringing their bells to sell goods. It was colourful, fascinating and, at times, a bit frightening.

Eventually we emerged from the warren of alleyways and came to the Jemaa el Fna square. By this time it was very busy and there were many more stalls. Several snake charmers were performing, but as soon as we approached them with cameras young boys rushed forward, shouting, "Dollars, dollars." They would not let anyone near the snake charmers unless money was forthcoming. I refused to pay, so I did not get any good pictures – only ones taken surreptitiously. I approached one group of people, but turned away as there was a cockfight in progress. In another area something unpleasant was happening to a sheep. I did not stop to investigate.

Having run the gauntlet of all the humanity in the square we went into the café for bottled drinks. Even here we were not safe from sellers of merchandise. Some of the older women wore yashmaks, but not many young ones wore them.

Back on the coach, having bid farewell to the local guide and tipped him handsomely, we were subject to a long lecture about education in Morocco and a further one on the Islamic religion. All we really wanted was to fall asleep.

After a while another coach passed us, although it was only a single-track road. Our Arab driver was so incensed he speeded up and made several attempts to get in front. When he did so, the other driver increased his speed and got ahead again, and the coaches rocked from side to side as the drivers, with lights flashing and horns blaring, tried to pass each other again and again.

Our port lecturer, Elwyn, was sitting in a front seat and was thrown into the stairwell near the driver. He yelled at him in English, then in Welsh, but to no avail. I had visions of us ending in a tangled mess. At last, the second coach pulled ahead, the driver sounding triumphant notes on his horn. The 'chariot race' was over. We had to stop at the next village as several passengers needed the loos after that experience.

It was getting cooler and as we went along we could see people kneeling by the roadside or in the fields. When we reached the outskirts of Casablanca it was quite dark. We were held up at the entrance to the dock area, as the police made the driver open the luggage bays for inspection. We travelled in the dark and rounded a corner to see the *Pacific Princess* lit up from stem to stern. It was a marvellous sight after a long day. One coach had arrived half an hour before and our lateness was causing some concern at the ship. Himself was waiting at the top of the gangway and seemed pleased to see me instead of a couple of camels.

That night the film in the cinema was *Casablanca*, but I was far too tired to watch it.

CHAPTER FOUR

CANBERRA

By the time we set foot aboard the *Canberra*, she was an old lady in ship years, and beginning to show her age, yet she had style and elegance and exuded the flavour of an older generation of vessels. Apart from the *QE2*, she was the last of the liners built for carrying passengers across the length and breadth of the oceans. She had conveyed the '£10 Poms' from Britain to start new lives in Australia. Moreover she had done her duty in the Falklands. Somewhere in the stern of one deck was a huge mural showing her return to Southampton, dirty, rusting and bedraggled, but she was surrounded by an armada of small ships which had gone out to welcome her home. For some reason the mural always brought a lump to my throat.

In those days a band played on the quayside (often the Royal Signals) and the passengers threw paper streamers as she pulled away.

Our first voyage on the *Canberra* was to Norway – the fiords and Spitzbergen. The scenery was spectacular as we sailed along Hardanger Fiord, and later encountered the Lilliehook and Kongsberg glaciers. In Magdalena Fiord we saw ice floes, seals and a couple of sea lions. At Trondheim we wandered ashore and later met an old man who was dying to tell someone that he had been on a railway journey to Hell and back, and had the ticket to prove the claim. He told us he had been stationed there after the war, helping to clear a German ammunition dump. We stopped at Narvik, the scene of a naval battle during the war. Hereabouts, the *Altmark* – a German ship – which was full of British prisoners of war was boarded by sailors from HMS *Cossack* and they were all released.

The cold wind blew straight from the North Pole as we approached Spitzbergen. I stood alone on the promenade deck at the stern of the ship. There was no land in sight, but the changing sea and sky patterns were fascinating. I stayed until I felt my blood must have nearly congealed in spite of layers of woollies and long johns.

One of the highlights was a trip in a five-seater seaplane from Bergen up north towards the Arctic Circle. We flew over mountains, lakes, fiords and glaciers. The sun shone and the views were stupendous. However, I was quite surprised how bumpy the take-off and landing on the water were; it felt as if we were bouncing on concrete.

On another voyage the *Canberra* docked at Livorno (formerly called Leghorn) and I boarded a coach for Pisa and Florence. In Pisa the Leaning Tower leaned in an alarming manner, yet from one angle it seemed to be straight. We were not allowed entry as long-term repairs were in progress.

On arrival in Florence we were taken high above the city to Michelangelo Square, where we had wonderful views. There was a copy of Michelangelo's statue of David. We visited the Piazza del Duomo, where the cathedral and Giotto's campanile soar up into the sky. The eleventh-century baptistry in San Giovanni was decorated with mosaics and the East Door was in bronze by Ghiberti, depicting scenes from the Old Testament. These were described by Michelangelo as the 'Gates of Paradise'. The Pitti Palace was full of fabulous paintings, and in the Piazza della Signoria we saw another copy of David, the original being kept indoors away from the elements. We passed the house where Robert and Elizabeth Browning lived. In the distance was the River Arno and the famous Ponte Vecchio with its goldsmiths' and silversmiths' shops. It was a long day, but an excellent tour.

Our cabins in the *Canberra* were always spacious as Himself insisted on having what he called 'decent accommodation', and we had to be amidships to avoid too much rocking and rolling in a storm. She was really a two-class ship, although the division was not always apparent. It was some time before we realised that passengers in cabins above a certain numeral dined in one restaurant and the rest dined in another. One was very luxurious and held fewer diners. The other was huge and canteen-like. One day, on my wanderings round the ship I discovered that the cabins on the lower decks had no portholes or showers or lavatories – these were along the passage. It was not quite the old saying 'God bless the squire and his relations and keep us in our proper stations', but there was a difference.

By the time we visited Odessa and Yalta, glasnost had been initiated and we felt more welcome than on our visit to Leningrad. We had passed through the Dardenelles, and Gallipoli was on our port side. There were many memorial stones and plaques on the hills and a huge Turkish one was floodlit every night. At Odessa, the sea was so rough we had to anchor and wait for a Russian pontoon to be towed to Canberra so that passengers could disembark on to Russian ferries. Our tenders could not be used in the weather conditions.

Odessa was known as the 'Hero City' as it had stood bravely against the Germans. There was a tall obelisk as a war memorial at the end of a tree-lined walk. Young cadets, male and female, from a nearby naval school, stood guard in turn at the memorial and eternal flame, twenty-four hours a day. Every hour a loudspeaker broadcast a poem to remind people of those who had sacrificed their lives.

We walked to the Potemkin Steps, passing the statue of Grigori Potemkin and the house where he lived. We passed the opera house, where I had hoped to see the ballet. Unfortunately not enough passengers aboard the *Canberra* wanted to buy tickets, so the event was cancelled.

As we wandered round the city, we were stopped occasionally by youths who pushed up the sleeves of their jackets, saying, "Want to buy a good watch?" and exposing two or three on an arm. Little old babushkas were sweeping the streets with dustpans and brushes while teenagers looked like ones the world over in miniskirts and jeans.

On the ship, Himself queued to buy postcards (nowadays they are often available about three days after we have left a particular port) and on my return there was time before the outgoing collection to write them, saying, naturally, 'From Russia with Love.'

Yalta was beautiful, surrounded by mountains, and in the early morning sun the little clouds were tinted pink. At the quayside was a big notice saying, "You are welcome" – more glasnost. In the coach we passed parks and gardens and numerous convalescent homes, used by workers sent from all over Russia to recover from illnesses.

The Livadia Palace, once a home of Tsar Nicholas II was the venue for the Yalta Conference. The conference room had been restored to how it was when Churchill, Roosevelt and Stalin met there. The walls were lined with photographs taken at the time. The grounds were attractive and the views were magnificent. The guide suggested that we visit the lavatories, which had been unlocked especially for our benefit. They were very clean and had mosaic-tiled walls and floors.

We went to the Swallow's Nest, the symbol of Yalta. It is a turreted castle perched on a cliff jutting out to sea. By the time we got to the Vorontsov Palace, where Churchill stayed during the conference, it was so hot that I opted to sit in the shade of the trees outside the building.

That evening we sailed back along the coastline past Sevastopol and the ruins of Inkerman, and we were a few miles south of Balaclava at one point – all names that made long-ago history come alive.

31

Most evenings Himself and I had a routine. We dressed for dinner before going to the casino, back to the restaurant for dinner and then on to a show or concert. Over the course of different cruises I had become addicted to the one-armed bandits in the casino. Himself used to play on the poker machines. I limited myself to 50 pence per night in those low-inflation days and I never won a jackpot. One evening I went to the cashier and handed over my money in exchange for ten 5-pence tokens. Himself followed behind me and the cashier, not realising that we were together, commented, "There goes the last of the big spenders."

What a history has Istanbul! The city was once known as Constantinople after the Emperor Constantine; before then it was the capital of the Byzantine and Ottoman empires. It was sacked during the Crusades and later captured by the Turks.

We went by coach over the Galatia Bridge into Old Istanbul and visited the Blue Mosque with its six minarets and huge domes. We left our shoes outside and were amazed at the breathtaking sight as we stepped indoors. The mosque is called 'blue' because of the thousands of blue tiles on the walls and domes. There were many tourists, but the people who were praying in the railed-off areas took no notice of them. The women in their black garments were segregated into areas at the back of the mosque. Outside in the grounds it was like a big marketplace, with vendors selling postcards, shawls, roses and food on trays. There were even people offering shoe-cleaning services.

We visited the Topkapi Palace through the Gate of the White Eunuchs. The Treasury was full of jewels and valuable artefacts, including the famous Topkapi Dagger. Among the exhibits was the purported arm of John the Baptist. It was a gruesome sight and of doubtful origin, I imagine. In the kitchen, where 200 cooks used to prepare meals for 5,000 people every day, there was a wonderful display of Chinese porcelain. On the other side of the courtyard was the harem, now empty. We had no time to visit the Hall of the Black

Eunuchs and the Courtyard of the Favourites.

From Topkapi we went to the ancient hippodrome, travelling in the coach along the track where the chariots had raced long ago. In the centre of the area were two obelisks, one from Egypt and the very ancient Serpent Column from Delphi.

On our way back to the ship we recrossed the Galatia Bridge and saw fishermen selling their wares from little boats. Others were sitting on the bridge fishing with rods and lines, oblivious of the noisy traffic. The *Canberra* was docked not far from the Florence Nightingale Hospital at Scutari – another name from the history books.

Years ago there was no doubt that the tours were excellent value. There was no doubt either that the *Canberra* was our kind of ship. She had high standards and kept to the old traditions, such as dressing for dinner every night, first-class entertainment and interdenominational church services on a Sunday. Here there were proper hymns with the correct tunes, readings from the King James Bible, and the national anthem. The collections from the large congregations were substantial and went to seamen's charities.

The dining-room and cabin staff, in latter years, were mainly Indian, many of them young, cheerful and eager for promotion. On one voyage we had a delightful cabin steward who took a paternal interest in us and always addressed us as 'Sahib' and 'Memsahib'.

The theatre company put on shows that were not brash and included plays and musicals from the London stage. I well remember them doing scenes from *Miss Saigon*. At the end, somehow, on a small stage, they re-enacted the final scene with the helicopter taking off from the American Embassy and those left behind trying to cling on to it. When the curtains closed the whole audience rose as one and the applause was deafening.

Yet we knew that the *Canberra*'s days were coming to an end. Those Who Know Best were already constructing huge blocks of apartments ready to launch them on the waves and calling them cruise ships.

A good friend sent us a copy of an eye-witness account of the *Canberra*'s final departure. 'All the beds and cabins were made up as they would have been for a cruise. The public rooms were immaculate with flower arrangements set out as usual.'

The *Canberra* may have been going out to the ship-breaker's yard in Pakistan, but the old lady went out in style.

CHAPTER FIVE

ALASKA VIA THE ROCKIES

Years of watching Westerns on the TV must have brainwashed me into thinking that Calgary would be a Wild West town. Perhaps I expected covered wagons racing through a wide street with wooden buildings on either side, and a saloon with horses hitched up to the rails outside. Gary Cooper lookalikes would be strolling around the precincts looking menacing if not exactly aggressive. Instead we flew into a modern airport and saw a skyline of high buildings, a bustling, vibrant place just like many other Canadian cities.

Sometimes we travelled with friends who enjoyed cruising. On this occasion our three good companions were Dorothy, Cynthia and Perce, whom we had known for many years. We were on our way through the Rockies to Vancouver to join the *Sky Princess* bound for Alaska.

We were escorted to a coach by a pleasant young Canadian guide and we travelled from Calgary to Banff and the Banff Springs Hotel. Here we were pleased to have a bath, a good meal and a restful night after the long plane journey. The hotel was built like a medieval castle and had some interesting architectural features. There were numerous Japanese tourists staying there; in fact, they were everywhere in the Rockies and in Alaska. I suppose this was natural because Japan is nearer the west coast of Canada than are the British Isles.

After leaving Banff we went through some breathtaking scenery to Lake Louise. Before getting there we stopped and went up in a ski lift to the top of a high peak. From there we had a view of the lake and the Victoria Glacier in the furthermost valley. Then we came down and went on to the Chateau Lake Louise Hotel. Our rooms had stunning views of the lake and mountains. The food was excellent and later we wandered in the grounds and round the shops, which seemed to be a feature of upmarket hotels in the area.

At 6 a.m. the next morning I was up and dressed and walking down by the lake. It was very quiet – no noise even from the numerous birds. I took a photograph of a porcupine.

From Lake Louise we took a trip to the Columbia Icefield. On the way we saw black bears and elks. We went on a snow coach to the Athabasca Glacier. It was bitterly cold and we had difficulty walking on the ice. Our guide gave us little cardboard cups to collect melting water from the glacier. Then he came round with a bottle of whisky and put a good measure in the water to warm us up. We picnicked in the coach at a later stop. The weather was wet and cold and too bad for the white-water rafting, so we went to our next destination.

Jasper in the pouring rain was not a welcoming sight. We had log cabins in the grounds of Jasper Park Lodge Hotel; and we were told that if we phoned through to the main building, transport would be provided to take us there for a meal.

A covered Jeep conveyed us through the downpour and we made our way to the dining room. It was here we discovered the drawbacks of using computers. Each group of tables had a computer terminal and the waitresses used them to communicate with the kitchen. Our young lady pushed the wrong buttons and our main course was ordered and cancelled twice. When the food did arrive it was not what we had ordered. Himself, much irritated, sent for the manager and suggested that the use of old-fashioned notepads and pencils might improve matters. Although it was in a beautiful setting

36

and was overlooked by Mount Cavell, named after Edith Cavell, we were not too thrilled with Jasper. This could have been owing to the very wet weather.

Over the Yellowhead Pass and following the North Thompson river we set off for Kamloops. We stopped near Mount Robson, the highest mountain in the Rockies, and had an excellent lunch. I tried, without much success, to photograph hummingbirds in the hotel grounds.

The owners of Hacienda Cabbello at Kamloops were very welcoming. It was a ranch-like farm with acres of gardens and grounds and a large lake. The weather was hot, but the environment was delightful and we had a good barbecue meal.

Vancouver was an adventure in itself, and we were fortunate to spend time in the city. We went over to Vancouver Island and saw many of the sights, including beautiful Stanley Park and Gardens. Eventually we boarded the *Sky Princess* for our voyage up the Inner Passage to Alaska.

The ship was similar to other *Princess* vessels on which we had travelled. All the waiters in the dining room and the maître d' were Italian. They tended to be a bit excitable, but the service was good and the food well up to the standard we expected.

As we sailed towards Juneau I saw my first whale. It surfaced close to the ship and revealed its huge forked tail as it dived. I am ashamed to say I shrieked with fright and surprise. After that we saw several whales and one or two dived quite close to us. At Juneau it was pouring with rain, but we were told it was good weather for whale-watching. We went on a wildlife trip in a glass-sided catamaran. We followed humpback whales and saw sea lions. On the shore were some brown bears with their cubs. Bald eagles festooned the trees on the shoreline. It was a memorable experience.

The next day was Dorothy's birthday. Himself delivered a card to their cabin, but did not tell her that he had ordered a cake to be presented to her at dinner. She was surprised but also embarrassed when a group of waiters gathered round to sing 'Happy Birthday'. This is a usual practice on cruise ships, the moral being never let anyone know you have a birthday when you are on board.

At Skagway we wandered through the town with its old buildings and tourist attractions. After lunch we went on the White Pass Yukon Railway up to the Canadian border. It was built in 1898–1900 as a route over the mountains to transport the gold miners to the Klondike. Many years ago the author Jack London wrote vivid accounts of the building of the railway, and the huge loss of life among men and horses. We passed several rudimentary graveyards at the side of the tracks.

Another day we spent sailing in Glacier Bay. The weather was sunny but very cold. When we reached the glacier, the Captain turned the ship and stopped the engines. At first it was very quiet, then from time to time we heard cracks and bangs as large pieces fell from the glacier and floated away as icebergs. As we went across the bay there were more whales cavorting in the water.

We docked at Sitka and went ashore by tender. The area is well known for the coniferous trees which grow in abundance. It was an interesting place and we spent some time wandering about and shopping. We saw some beautiful huskies round the town.

Finally we sailed back to Vancouver and were taken to an hotel to wait until it was time to be conveyed to the airport for our ten-hour flight home. It was warm and sunny and we had a last look around the city. It has many fine buildings and a large harbour. It was discovered by Captain George Vancouver in 1792.

Eventually we were taken to the airport, but the journey home was a shambles. The flight was an hour late and the food was awful. I opened a container at dinner, looked at the mess inside and handed it back to the stewardess. The intercom did not work properly, so we could not hear any announcements. Before we took off, some Asian ladies refused to sit in the seats allocated to them because they wanted to sit with their relations. The stewardess, instead of politely asking them to sit in their seats, went round asking passengers to move and make room. Nobody would give up a seat, so we were held up another half-hour until the problem was solved.

Tired and hungry, we arrived at Heathrow the next morning. After the cold weather in the Rockies and Alaska we found the heat in London overpowering. Yet, in spite of the tiresome journey home, we all agreed that it had been an unforgettable experience.

Chapter Six

ORIANA

Himself and I have never been on a maiden voyage, thinking – perhaps wrongly – that a new ship is like a new car and needs time to settle down and iron out the gremlins. Consequently it was a year or so before we embarked on the *Oriana*.

Rumour had it that she was similar to the *Canberra*, but this was not the case. She was beautiful and had her own ambience with spacious cabins, impressive public rooms and restaurants, and a theatre which was arranged so that every seat had a clear view of the stage.

The library was well equipped with books which nestled on shelves designed by David Linley. The lovely hexagonal table in the centre, the longcase clock in the Thackeray Room next door and other items were by the same designer. Gone were the days when books were taken out and returned at leisure. There was a qualified librarian, who checked each volume in and out on a computer.

One of the most impressive public areas was the Curzon Room, a huge lounge ringed with comfortable armchairs. In the centre was a raised platform on which rested a grand piano. It was here that we often gathered to listen to classical concerts.

The *Oriana* was our favourite ship for many years. Even

apart from a world cruise, we travelled thousands of sea miles on her – from Venice to the Virgin Islands, from Quebec to Singapore and countless ports in between. She was sleek and stylish and she looked like a proper ship, being built just before the 'apartment-look syndrome' had caught on.

Our first voyage on her was up to the North Cape. On this occasion we were with our friends Norah and Malcolm, who had been cruising for longer than we had. Cynthia joined us and we had an hilarious time together.

The Stadium Theatre Company put on some excellent performances in those days. We became friendly with Alison, an assistant cruise entertainments director who was also an entertainer and who appeared in some of the productions.

One afternoon we three girls met her outside the theatre and she took us on a tour backstage. We saw the lavish costumes and the dressing areas, and she explained how the revolving stage worked. It was an interesting afternoon – a real peep behind the scenes.

Sometimes we went on 'themed' cruises, which then signified top-class entertainment. We were on one of the musical cruises when Richard Baker was on board with singers and instrumentalists. Not only did we listen to enjoyable music in the evenings, ranging from Beethoven to Gilbert and Sullivan, and later composers, but we attended interesting lectures in the mornings or afternoons. On another themed cruise, 'Antiques', we enjoyed lectures by Hilary Kay, Paul Atterbury and members of the *Antiques Roadshow* team. Many of their anecdotes were very amusing.

A Christmas and New Year cruise on the *Oriana* was an interesting experience. This time we were back on board with Dorothy and Perce. The weather in the Channel was stormy – a force-9 gale prevailed in the Bay of Biscay. There were no Health & Safety rules in place, so the decks were not closed off. I was able to go to the stern and watch the storm. Fortunately, none of us were ever seasick, but in such circumstances sick bags were placed around the ship. Nowadays euphemisms abound, so they are labelled 'For Motion Disturbance'.

The gale grew to force 11 and at Madeira we had to wait outside Funchal Harbour for nearly five hours. All tours were cancelled and several passengers flew home, having had enough of rough seas.

Eventually we reached calm waters, and St Kitts in the Caribbean was our first port of call. Our tour revealed the island's violent past. Many places had been fought over by British and French troops. At Bloody Point they had united to massacre 3,000 Caribbean natives in 1626. A giant tamarind tree marked the dividing point formerly separating parts of the island under British and French rule.

On Christmas Eve we docked at Dominica and we went on a rainforest tour. We drove through steep forested hills and saw some very unusual trees – mahot cochon, cre cre, kaklin and others. Tree orchids, huge poinsettias and coleuses grew wild by the roadside.

Back on the ship, which was beautifully decorated, we had Christmas Eve dinner. Later we exchanged presents with Dorothy and Perce and all agreed we should give our dining and cabin stewards some extra money for Christmas.

On Christmas Day we went to a 'Service of Nine Lessons and Carols'. Himself, having been persuaded by our friend Alison, the entertainments director, was in the choir. There was a happy, festive atmosphere on board and the *Oriana* sailed through calm waters.

At Bridgetown, Barbados, we went out in an adapted submarine or Seatrack vessel for an underwater view of marine life. We saw a number of fishes, but not as many as we had expected to encounter.

By this time Himself had established a habit of ensconcing himself on the ship while my friends and I went ashore. However, at Bridgetown he broke his routine and the two of us took a taxi out to see the Kennington Oval cricket ground. We negotiated the fare for a return journey and waiting time,

$10 (US), which we thought was reasonable.

It was a dilapidated vehicle; the seat belts did not pull and the doors could only be opened from the outside, probably to stop people from running off without paying. We went through some of the less salubrious parts of Bridgetown and got to the ground only to find it closed for renovations. The taxi driver went round the back and found an opening in the fence, through which we squeezed.

The area was much smaller than we expected, but we took photographs, especially of the three stands named after three great cricketers – Worrell, Walcott and Weekes.

Grenada was very hot and the tour to Flamboyant Beach was disappointing, although the scenery was exotic.

St Lucia with its volcanic spires, Gros Piton and Petit Piton, rising up to the skies was more interesting. A few of us went to the Marquis Plantation, once the estate of the French governor. We drove through areas of cedar, teak and mahogany trees, banana plantations and breadfruit trees. There were mangoes, guavas and, alongside the road, oleander, tamarisk and tulip trees. It was like paradise.

There was a demonstration of Creole cookery in antique pots and then we went in a flat-bottomed boat down the Marquis River to the Atlantic coast.

Back at the house we had a buffet lunch of chicken, salads and a banana bread pudding. There was a choice of rum, sorrel or coconut drinks. Our guide was a middle-aged lady who was very knowledgeable and kept drawing our attention to the flora and fauna and the history of the island. This was one of the best tours we had ever taken.

On New Year's Eve the haggis was piped in, followed by a lady purser carrying two crossed bottles of whisky. Burns' poem 'To a Haggis' was recited. At midnight the Captain counted down to the minute and then the oldest sailor on board, the coxswain, and the youngest, a cadet, rang the old year out and the New Year in with eight bells. There was much hilarity and we enjoyed watching the Captain and some of the officers dancing Scottish reels.

As we headed northwards, the weather started to deteriorate. By the time we reached Vigo it was cold and wet and stormy. Two couples decided to fly home from there, which was a good move. The Captain spoke of atrocious conditions ahead and warned everyone to be careful. We ran into a force-12 gale with huge waves.

The heavy filing cabinet in Alison's office fell on to its side with a crash. Huge pots with Christmas trees in them were flung around like toys. After one big lurch, perfume displays, watches and clothes in the shops were hurled around and the shops were closed.

So ended our Christmas and New Year cruise on the *Oriana*, but it did not detract from the pleasure of the places we had visited and the experiences of the voyage.

We had many more enjoyable voyages on her: we crossed the Atlantic to New York and Boston, went down the Eastern Seaboard of America, visited George Washington's home at Mount Vernon, went in flat-bottomed boats looking for alligators in the Okefenokee Swamp, and called at Williamsburg and other towns in what seemed like 'Scarlett O'Hara country'.

On another occasion we left the *Oriana* at New York and spent a week exploring New England, visiting Kennebunkport and going across to Martha's Vineyard, among other fascinating places.

It was because of the interesting itineraries and happy memories that we decided to embark on the *Oriana* for a three-month world cruise.

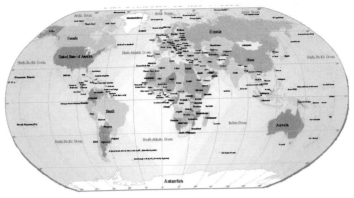

CHAPTER SEVEN

ROUND THE WORLD

On a bitterly cold night in early January we stood on the deck of the *Oriana* as she slipped away from the quayside and sailed down Southampton Water at the beginning of her world cruise. Himself never gets excited about such matters, but I was amazed to think that in my twilight years I was going to see all the places about which I had dreamed.

After a couple of days at sea, I went to a lecture given by John McCarthy, the 'Port Lecturer'. He was an American, and we had encountered him on previous voyages. He was an excellent speaker, clear, factual and amusing. He did not advertise any particular tour, but gave a history of the place to be visited, and illustrated it with his own colourful slides. Passengers flocked to his lectures, many of them sitting in the aisles when all the seats in the theatre or cinema were taken. He also gave lectures on topics of special interest during days at sea.

Later in the day we had to hand in our passports, yellow-fever certificates and various papers to be checked against the passenger list. At night a group of classical singers performed in one of the lounges. They were good and the Welsh tenor was outstanding.

An early port of call was St Vincent in the Cape Verde

Islands. I wandered ashore and, after admiring some of the architecture, I spent a few dollars – a small contribution to the local economy. How strange it is that the Americans are unjustifiably vilified round the world, yet the dollar is the currency that people try to get their hands on.

When we reached the equator we went to watch the crossing-the-line ceremony in the bows of the ship. Himself had crossed this particular line on several occasions, both during and after the war, but he was persuaded to attend. It was a noisy affair and when King Neptune and his entourage arrived, and the Captain's team appeared, some of the audience yelled and shouted like a football crowd. Having seen and heard as much as we wanted, we slipped away to a quieter part of the ship.

After crossing the equator we were buffeted by the trade winds and we saw neither ship nor bird until we made landfall at Walvis Bay, Namibia. As there was little transport, the coaches had to be brought from Windhoek. On our tour we stopped at Walvis Bay Lagoon and saw hundreds of flamingoes and pelicans. We went on to the dunes and stopped at Dune 7, the highest sand dune in the area. A few foolhardy people started to climb the sandy slopes, but they did not get far. We continued through the Namib Desert to Swakopmund, a town full of nineteenth-century architecture, a legacy of German colonial days. Everywhere was so clean – no rubbish or graffiti. The guide told us that anyone who dropped litter was fined on the spot. If they could not pay, they were taken away by 'men in suits' to do compulsory work. What a pity they do not have such arrangements in the UK!

As we approached Cape Town I was up at about 6 a.m. to see Robben Island, where Nelson Mandela was imprisoned. Table Mountain loomed ahead enveloped in mist; the locals call this mist 'the Tablecloth'.

The next day was fine and sunny, so it was possible to take a cable car to the top of the mountain. This was an amazing experience. The car, or rather the floor of the car, rotated through 360 degrees on the four-minute journey and the views were spectacular. Near to the top it seemed as if we would crash into the huge rocks and cliffs. The journey down was just as exciting.

On this tour I acquired a gentleman friend – George, an elderly Australian. We went up in the cable car and wandered together at the top of Table Mountain. In the coach on the way back to the ship we talked about cricket and books. This was a pleasant change as, being on my own, I find that the person sitting next to me is often a latter-day Ancient Mariner, who tells me more than I need to know about his health or fellow passengers. George was great fun and he, Himself and I met up on numerous occasions until he left the ship at Melbourne.

The huge harbour at Durban was so big that helicopters criss-crossed it all day instead of ferries. We reached the Tala Game Reserve in coaches, but transferred to open vehicles in which we bumped along track roads. We saw many species of animals – hippos, rhinos, giraffes, zebras, wildebeests and other antelopes, including the rare sable antelope. Some of the animals, even the warthog, moved very quickly. One interesting stop was at a tree hung with nests of weaver birds. The bright-yellow males were sitting near the nests to tempt the females to enter.

My fellow passengers in the truck were armed with high-tech cameras and they were too free with their elbows, pushing to get a good position whenever we stopped. I reckoned David Attenborough did not have to put up with that sort of behaviour on his safaris.

I had forgotten how hot Africa can be. We docked at Mombasa at 7 a.m. and the temperature was in the eighties. I had wanted to go to the Amboseli National Park in the shadow of Kilimanjaro. However, as there had recently been terrorist attacks on an hotel in Mombasa and an aircraft, Himself put so much pressure on me not to go that I had to give way. Consequently I had to be content with wandering ashore accompanied by Himself, as self-appointed guard dog. Mombasa was very underwhelming, although we could see the magnificent beaches on the far side of the bay. There was an impressive double arch of elephant tusks across Moi Avenue. They were actually made of sheet metal, but looked like the real thing.

While we were in port the security arrangements had an Alice in Wonderland feeling about them. Along the narrow quayside were warehouses and a building with a balcony. On the balcony were two chairs and a couple of armed soldiers took it in turns to gaze at the ship. On the second day the one on duty was fast asleep, nursing his Kalashnikov rifle like a baby. At the open dockyard gates, beyond the stern of the ship, the sentry had left his post and wandered off to talk to a man who was fishing. No doubt it did not matter as the area was so quiet – no shipping, no little boats bobbing about, no tankers. In fact there was no movement at all, except for an occasional police launch which trundled up and down past the *Oriana*. At least one hoped the mooring fees of a ship her size would help the economy.

Port Victoria in the Seychelles was lush and green, but the rain did not help to make a lasting impression. Only the giant tortoises and the flying foxes created much interest.

From here we were six days at sea – spent reading and relaxing and attending several lectures by John McCarthy. At night we listened to classical music or played cards.

The night before we docked at Penang, I got ready for a tour. It was like planning an expedition to the Sahara: tour tickets, money, cruise card (for checking on and off the ship), reading glasses, comb, make-up, tissues, camera, sunglasses, sunblock, hat, insect repellent and a bottle of water. I nearly forgot to add the binoculars to the pile.

At Penang we were taken off the ship in the tenders. By the time we reached the coaches the temperature was ninety degrees. George Town, the capital, looked prosperous with skyscrapers and luxury hotels, taller than some in New York. We visited a butterfly farm, which was also a home to green iguanas and other lizards, scorpions, snakes and huge koi fish.

When we returned to George Town we visited the Buddhist temple of Wat Chayamangkalaram, which houses a reclining Buddha 108 feet long called the Smiling Buddha. It seemed to be made of painted cement with eyes and toenails of pearl. I did not care for it, but it is a question of beauty being in the eye of the beholder.

The next day in Kuala Lumpur (KL) it was all mosques and minarets and amazing futuristic buildings. On the way there we passed the Blue Mosque, but it was not as impressive as the one in Istanbul.

It was all very well for Himself and others on board to be blasé about Singapore, but for someone like me, who had never been east of Suez before, it was a fascinating place. I took the first shuttle bus from the quayside into the city and was surprised to see so much greenery – trees, shrubs and grassy areas – along the roads and streets. I wandered about and got on an escalator which took me to a bridge to cross Scotts Road. Then I set off for Orchard Road, the main shopping centre. I was accosted three times on the way – twice by men offering me a taxi and what the third wanted I knew not, but I thanked them all politely and declined their offers. I reckoned I was a bit too ancient for the white-slave market.

In the afternoon I went on an interesting coach tour of the city, and then to the Raffles Hotel for afternoon tea. The place was big and impressive. Although aficionados say it has lost its character, the hotel, the polite staff and the magnificent tea certainly impressed me.

Later we were free to wander round the complex with its large, expensive shops. I went outside the buildings and had a look round the Chinese quarter. Himself would have objected if he had seen me there on my own, but it felt quite safe, only the traffic was a menace.

Before we sailed we watched the cable cars moving continually from the World Trade Centre to Sentosa Island. It had been a memorable day.

The next day we crossed the equator for the third time and

then had several days at sea before we reached Fremantle. Many passengers spent time and money in the shops. There was such an array of goods on offer: watches, jewellery, bags, clothing, Royal Doulton ware and crystal.

I chatted with a sweet old American lady and she told me about her purchases. "Honey, I have bought just about everything – Royal Doulton, crystal, Wedgwood, jewellery . . . I've shopped until I am exhausted."

"But you will have to pay an awful lot of duty when you go through customs at home," I said.

"Duty? Oh no, we seniors don't ever get stopped at the customs," she replied.

"Never?" I asked, incredulous.

"No! I mean, it wouldn't look good if we were stopped and searched and something happened, would it?"

"If something happened?" I asked.

"Well, supposing one of our party had a heart attack? Or a fatal collapse? It wouldn't look good in the papers – 'Senior Citizens Harassed by Customs' – would it? No, they just wave us through and we all go right along."

I often wonder if things might have changed these days, even for seniors.

Fremantle was a delightful city. On our tour we stopped at the Round House, an old twelve-sided jail, and saw Pensioner Forces Cottages, which once housed a British garrison. I wandered off to admire the old Esplanade Hotel and the Fremantle Maritime Museum. We travelled along the banks of the Swan river to Perth, the capital of Western Australia. In King's Park, at the top of Mount Eliza, were the Western Australian Botanical Gardens and a moving state war memorial for the fallen of two world wars. On our way back to Fremantle we stopped at Lake Monger to see the lovely black swans and their broods.

About an hour and a half before we sailed, crowds of people gathered on a wide balcony along the dockside building. There were streamers, balloons and banners, and a brass band played.

As the ship pulled away a huge roar went up. People waved and cheered and shouted, "Bon voyage!" and the *Oriana's* siren hooted continuously in farewell. As we passed along the harbour wall there were more crowds of people cheering and waving and again the ship's siren hooted in reply. It was a heart-warming send-off from Fremantle. The weather was atrocious as we crossed the Great Australian Bight.

At Melbourne we both bade farewell to George, our Australian friend, who had been such a good companion on the voyage since we met in Cape Town. We promised to keep in touch when we returned to England.

After a tour of the city, seeing among other sights Captain Cook's Cottage and the Melbourne Cricket Ground, we crossed the Yarra river and went out to the Dandenongs. Here were white cockatoos, rosellas and king parrots. We heard bellbirds and lyrebirds, but did not see them. At Olinda we stopped at the Cuckoo Restaurant (Swiss clocks everywhere) and had coffee with delicious scones.

In Tasmania, we went on the long trip to the heart of the country, where there were beautiful lakes, forests and mountains. The Trowunna Wildlife Park, Mole Creek, was a highlight. It was a conservation and breeding centre for koala bears (not native in Tasmania) and in many acres of bushland were kangaroos, wallabies, wombats and Tasmanian devils. Several koala bears were asleep, cradled round the branches of gum trees. I managed to take a few photographs, including one of a kookaburra and some white cockatoos.

Wherever we went in Tasmania the people were very friendly and helpful, and made us feel at home.

The ship was given a good send-off with a brass band and a crowd of locals. I guess most of the passengers would leave with very warm feelings towards the lovely people and country of Tasmania.

I opened the curtains one morning later and the Sydney Opera House loomed straight in front of the cabin window. The Sydney Harbour Bridge (nicknamed 'the coat hanger') was on the starboard side of the ship. Himself decided to come ashore with me, and we explored parts of the city together. Eventually he headed back to the *Oriana* and I set off at a spanking pace for the quayside and boarded one of the green-and-yellow ferries to cross the harbour to Manly. It was a delightful place and the water near the quayside was so clear that I could see shoals of fish. I would have liked to stay at Manly for a good while, but knew I must return lest Himself became too worried by my absence. As it turned out, he was quite concerned that I had spent the 'getting-lost money', which was supposed to be used for a taxi to bring me back to the ship in case of an emergency.

After lunch I got ready to go on a tour of the opera house and to an evening performance of *Orpheus in the Underworld*. The dress code was listed as 'semi-formal' so I wore a smart trouser suit. Some of the ladies wore evening gowns and were dripping with jewels. After an interesting walk all round the building, we were left to get some food and warned to be in our seats promptly because the doors would be closed exactly on time. Nobody was allowed in late; those who were late arriving had to wait in the foyer until the first interval. In the foyer was a television screen where latecomers could watch the action on stage. Apparently many VIPs had been obliged to use that facility. Nowadays, every time I hear music from *Orpheus in the Underworld* I am back in Sydney Opera House among that packed enthusiastic audience.

After Australia we encountered choppy seas on the way to New Zealand. However, once we entered Marlborough Sounds the water was calm and the words 'spectacular' and 'stunning' were scarcely adequate to describe the scenery.

A grand piano had been transported to Deck 8 Aft and the resident pianist played classical music as we drifted towards Picton. Every chair on the decks overlooking the pianist was taken and many passengers were standing. It was a peaceful scene. Obviously not all the onlookers were enraptured as I heard one woman say to another as they stood behind me,

"How much does your hairdresser charge for a shampoo and set?"

When we docked at Lyttelton, Himself and I took a shuttle bus into town, where we were met by our old friends Brenda and Jim. It was good to see them after an interval of many years.

We headed off for Christchurch and a packed day of sightseeing. The International Antarctic Centre was fascinating and we spent some time there. Afterwards we went out to Brenda and Jim's lovely home with its colourful garden and had lunch. We chatted on the phone to Brenda's sister Beryl (my friend in Canada) and her husband, Jim, also my cousin Betty and her husband, Wray, who were visiting them. I felt quite emotional at all their kindness.

Then it was back to the city and Hagley Park and the botanical gardens. The begonia house was a mass of colourful blooms.

We declined an invitation to climb the ninety steps to the top of the Anglican cathedral designed by Sir George Gilbert Scott. In Cathedral Square was a statue of John Robert Godley, the founder of the city named after his Oxford college. There was so much to see and our friends made it a very special day. That evening we got the young librarian to send them an e-mail to convey our thanks.

At Auckland the coaches left the ship at 7.30 a.m. and we travelled for three hours to Rotorua. On the way the sky turned black, lightning ripped across the area and the rain came down in stair rods. No wonder the country was so lush and green with such storms! Perhaps the weather affected my judgement because, although the boiling mud pools, hot springs and spouting geysers were impressive, I thought they were not as dramatic as those in Iceland.

After lunch we went to the Agrodome and entered a large building with a stage at one end. One by one, like chorus girls, a specimen of each of the nineteen breeds of sheep raised in New Zealand went up to their individual stands. At the apex was a huge merino, the star of the show. Unperturbed they all sat or stood and gazed at the audience. We watched a sheep-shearing demonstration. There was a cow which members of the audience were invited to milk, and a lamb-feeding competition with the winner being given the fleece of the sheared sheep.

There were more days at sea and one of them was Groundhog Day. Revealing my ignorance, I asked a young man at the Tours Office what it meant. Patiently he explained that it was the antipode where the two hemispheres met and the dates changed. In order to correct the time changes we repeat one day.

There were very few top-class artistes on the cruise, much to the annoyance of the 400 or so round-the-worlders on board (other passengers got on and off at various stages). Allan Schiller, the world-famous pianist, was one, and Pam Ayres was another, but their stays on board were brief and their performances were packed – evidence that people do appreciate quality. First-class lecturers like John McCarthy attract huge audiences, as do top performers.

Having recently read some of Nevil Shute's novels, I was looking forward to seeing Papeete, which features in *The Trustee from the Toolroom*. I envisaged a sleepy little place not much altered from his description, written over fifty years ago. In reality it was a thriving port and a town heaving with traffic. Another dream was shattered.

Bora Bora was one of the most beautiful places we visited. We anchored in the lagoon and by 8.30 a.m. the temperature was in the nineties. We were taken ashore by tender and I went on an excursion in a glass-bottomed boat to see the fish life. Through large glass panels at our feet we saw myriads of different species, including parrotfish, butterfly fish, sturgeon, trumpet fish and many more. As the boat eased along there were huge sea anemones and more brilliantly coloured fish darting in and out of the coral. A giant eel dived from its hiding place and seized a fish to eat.

On shore, whichever way we wandered, the scenery was beautiful. Bora Bora is believed to have been the inspiration for Bali Ha'i in the musical *South Pacific*.

At Lahaina, capital of Maui, Hawaii, there were whales playing between the ship and the shore while we were having breakfast. The US immigration officers came aboard and passengers had to have their passports stamped and papers inspected in the Curzon Room. We went ashore by tender and found Lahaina was a pleasant little town with a background of mountains. After some sightseeing I gravitated to the shops, where there were many Hawaiian shirts. I was determined to get one for Himself. He is a most non-acquisitive person and never wants anything for himself. I bought a colourful garment, but used up all my dollars, so went back to the quayside to catch a tender. Here I was thoroughly frisked and had to show my passport, cruise card and purchases to armed security guards. On the way back to the ship a whale popped up quite close to the tender. The helmsman kindly stopped the boat and the three of us (the only passengers) watched the creature playing and frolicking in the water, and admired its great tail as it dived and dived again.

As we sailed into Honolulu, dolphins swam alongside the ship as if guiding her into port. The visit to Pearl Harbor was a very moving experience. The *Arizona* Memorial is built across the mid section of the sunken vessel in which 1,177 men are entombed. On the lawn at the rear of the *Arizona* Visitor's Centre there is a stone circle with the names of all the men who died on that December day in 1941.

We watched a film depicting the Pearl Harbor attack. It was introduced by one of the survivors, who was in his eighties. The film gave some sad statistics. Twenty-three pairs of brothers were killed, and in half a dozen cases three brothers from one family died. At the end of the film there was no sound in the cinema and everyone walked out in silence. Legend has it that oil is still leaking from the *Arizona* and will continue to do so until the last survivor has died.

On the way back to the ship we went to the Punchbowl National Cemetery for American servicemen. It included the Courts of the Missing, remembering over 36,000 unknown warriors who were killed in various battlefields of the Pacific.

After more days at sea we docked at San Francisco. From the stern we could see Alcatraz and the Golden Gate Bridge. While waiting for a ferry to get across to Alcatraz, we could see and hear many sea lions which resided in K Dock, part of Pier 39. We were given a talk about the history and layout of the island by a National Ranger as it is a national park. I bought maps and a pamphlet about former inhabitants, who include Al Capone, George Kelly and Robert (the Birdman) Stroud. I meandered about this historic fortress on my own and found it fascinating.

On returning to the mainland and our coach, we were taken to Fisherman's Wharf with its variety of seafood stalls, restaurants and shops. On we went up and down San Francisco's steep streets and saw cable cars climbing to the top of them.

It was a big thrill to cross the Golden Gate Bridge on our way to the artists' colony of Sausalito. We recrossed it on our return journey. By the time we sailed in the evening it was raining, so we went up to the crow's nest to see the ship pass under the bridge. We could not see Alcatraz in the gloom, but the beam from the lighthouse there shone out bright and clear.

A few more days at sea helped me to restore my spent vitality after what Himself termed 'gallivanting' about Alcatraz and San Francisco.

At Acapulco it was very hot, already in the eighties when we set off on our tour. We stopped at the Hotel El Mirador and watched the famous cliff divers – The Clavadistas – dive off the jagged rocks into a narrow ravine at La Quebrada. The divers seemed to fly out beyond the cliffs before diving down into the water. After single displays they all dived together. As we were leaving the hotel, the divers lined up and a man was collecting tips. Most people put in something. I gave $8, one for each man, but a few folks walked past without any acknowledgement. Sometimes I despair of my fellow humans.

At Balboa we stayed overnight to await our journey through the Panama Canal early the next day. The fifty-one mile, nine-hour journey through the Pedro Miguel Locks and across the Gatun Lake to the Gatun Locks and out to the Caribbean Sea was a remarkable experience. We spent most of the day on deck in spite of the terrific heat. Even Himself was impressed by such a feat of engineering.

The *Oriana* was raised some seventeen metres above the Pacific, and there seemed to be only inches of leeway on either side of the ship. She went through a narrow channel to the Gaillard Cut and into Gatun Lake. There were jungly islands in the distance and the jungle came down to the water's edge. Alligators could be seen on the shore from time to time. We descended twenty-six metres to sea level in three stages before cruising the seven miles to Cristóbal and out into the Caribbean Sea on the way to Cartagena.

Cartagena, Columbia, was once one of the two strongest-fortified cities in the Americas, the other being Quebec. The old walled city with its winding streets and Spanish colonial architecture was very pleasant. The fortress of San Felipe de Barajas was massive. It was built over a period of 126 years and finished in 1657.

We saw the Church of the Slaves, the Plaza de Bolivar with a statue of Simon Bolivar, and the cathedral, which suffered when Francis Drake sacked the town.

The trade winds buffeted us to Aruba from Cartagena. The island has brilliant white sandy beaches and a lack of high-rise buildings, which was a pleasant change. The ubiquitous divi-divi (watapana) tree has its branches bent at right angles to the trunk by the wind.

At Barbados there was an excellent tour to Harrison's Cave with its network of huge caverns, streams and waterfalls, stalactites and stalagmites. Later we went to Orchid World, where there were over 30,000 orchids. I was very envious when I saw some of the exotic blooms, having spent twenty years on and off trying to cultivate orchids only to have them die on me. Obviously I did not provide the right ambience.

Our days at sea before we made our last landfall at the Azores were brightened with lectures by a man called Mike Craig. He had written many TV and radio shows. Here, at last, we had a funny man. He entertained everyone for over an hour without being blue or vulgar. Alongside John McCarthy with his port and special-interest lectures, he was first class.

In those days the Azores were not on the tourist map. The weather was damp and misty, so we did not see the Crater Lakes, one bright blue and the other bright green. We all bought postcards of what we should have seen.

A force-7 gale prevailed throughout our last two days at sea, but there were no sick bags in sight. Packing has always been a nightmare for me, but strangely enough not for Himself. When all was stowed away I sat on the bed and realised that we had actually been round the world. My enjoyment would have been much diminished without Himself, who put up with my enthusiasms and listened patiently to every detail of my tours. We had very few complaints during the cruise. The ship had been immaculate, the crew had worked hard and were always cheerful and the food was superb. The entertainment was, like the curate's egg, good in parts. The passengers were the usual mix of humanity – some delightful and others greedy and selfish.

There was the usual kind of one-upmanship among some who asked, "Have you been on many cruises?"

The reply would come: "Yes, this is my tenth."

Whereupon the questioner would say, "Really? This is my fifteenth."

Mike Craig, a great character, told many good jokes. One was the story of a lady, seated at a dining table, who asked her neighbour, "How many cruises have you done?"

"Five," he replied.

"I've done twelve," she informed him, before asking the

same question of her other neighbour.

He hesitated before saying, "Over 500. I've lost count."

She gasped, "That must have cost you a pretty penny!"

"No, it hasn't cost me anything, madam. I'm the chief engineer."

Happy days.

CHAPTER EIGHT

QE2

By the time Himself and I boarded the *QE2* she was in her last season. Like her, we were getting on in years, so we booked cabins in the Princess Grill. This meant we could be assured of our own table for two at every meal and could go to the dining room at any time during a two-and-a-half-hour span. No more waiting outside the doors at breakfast and lunchtime to dash in and get a suitable table!

The cabin was spacious with plenty of drawers, ample wardrobe space and a shower and bath. It had something we had not seen for years – portholes. Nice touches were a bottle of champagne on ice, a dish of strawberries with a bowl of sugar, a large bowl of fruit and a lovely flower arrangement.

There was a feeling of space and elegance about the ship. It reminded us of the *Canberra*, no doubt because they were both the last of the old liners as opposed to cruise ships. The Grill dining rooms were much smaller and more intimate than the restaurants. At dinner on the first night I had to change from a chosen dish as it contained garlic, to which I am very allergic. Within minutes the waiter had alerted the maître d', who came and assured me that I could choose anything and it would be cooked separately without garlic. From then onward, menus were brought to me each evening and I marked the dishes of choice for the next day.

Dollars were the currency if any onboard transactions were needed. Purchases in shops were signed for and went on the bill along with the tips. I went along to the purser's office – no reception area on this ship – to get some euros for going ashore. I was directed to a Dalek-like machine and could not make it work. A pleasant young woman came from the counter and it soon spat out the required amount.

We were amazed at the cosmopolitan composition of the crew, drawn from the United Kingdom, Australia, Canada, South Africa, Thailand, the Philippines and various other far-flung places. The same diversity applied to the passengers, with thirteen nationalities on board.

At Bilbao I took a tour to Guernica. The guide was very informative and at times more amusing than she realised. We stopped at a viewpoint to look at a small shrine to St James. She said there used to be a fortification on the spot, but it was destroyed by an English pirate called Francis Drake. I reckoned that was a good description of him. Later at Bermeo, a fishing town with a harbour full of Spanish boats, she said there were constant quarrels with the French, who were always overfishing. Seeing that it was the Spanish who had all but destroyed the English fishing industry, that had to be a joke.

At Guernica we were told about the Assembly House, the oak-tree symbol, the national jal-alai (handball) court, the park and gardens and finally the bombing of the city on 26 April 1937. I suppose that to a young woman 1937 was as far away as the Hundred Years War. Apparently Picasso did not allow his painting to return to Spain until Franco died.

We spent ninety minutes going round the Assembly House and Chamber and watching a video about the town and the oak-tree symbol. We were saturated with information and in need of what the guide termed 'The Necessarium'. We walked across the park to find that the loos were closed. As a result, the driver had to stop at the first service station and wait while everyone stampeded off the coach.

As the *QE2* left the harbour at Bilbao she gave several long blasts on her whistle to say goodbye, as it was her last time of calling at that port.

During the night the ship seemed to be moving at an alarming speed. One of the officers told us that, in spite of her forty years, she was still the fastest ship afloat. "She can go faster astern than some younger ships can go forward," he asserted.

One afternoon I went to the Queen's Room for tea, which was served by waiters in white jackets, black trousers and white gloves. There were several different kinds of sandwiches, scones with cream and jam, and delicious little cakes. Tea or coffee was on offer and each waiter lifted the cups from the table and put them on a tray on his arm so that nothing was spilled. I sat with an elderly lady and listened to a potted history of her many years of cruising with Cunard. I remarked that the room seemed quite full. She said sharply that it was because people from the Caronia and Mauretania restaurants were there. "They are not supposed to use the Queen's Room for tea. They should go up to the Lido where they belong," she declared.

In contrast, at Funchal I went for afternoon tea at Reid's Palace, which was famous because of its guests (including royalty, Churchill and numerous film stars) and its food. We were admitted through the hallowed portals by uniformed staff, who no doubt checked our attire to see that it was 'smart formal'.

The atmosphere was hushed and reverential. The tea was good, but not as good as that served in the Queen's Room on board ship. We had one scone each with jam and cream, three small sandwiches and two small cakes. Teapots were put on the table for us to pour our own. The scone was very good, so, not wanting sandwiches, I asked for another one and got a snooty look from the waiter. At the price we paid, I felt I deserved a second one and I got it.

An elderly lady joined me and ordered the waiter to bring

some fresh tea. He replied that the pot was still hot and got a reprimand, so he hurried off to replace it. In the course of conversation she mentioned Raffles Hotel and I recalled an enjoyable visit there several years ago.

"Not what it was!" she snapped.

Apparently she had stayed there recently and had flown back to join the *QE2* in her last season. Then she intended to fly to South America.

"I do think that at my age one must have something to which one can look forward," she declared. I ventured to ask her age and she replied, "I am ninety-three if it is any of your business."

As we left Madeira the *QE2* was accompanied by boats and she gave a series of long, loud blasts in farewell.

When we left Tenerife there was a big firework display to mark the occasion. At Las Palmas, Gran Canaria, a large number of vintage and veteran cars lined up on the quayside. There were some gorgeous models, including a lovely cream Packard and an early Jowett. One of the marshals said fifty cars were expected and they would stage a grand parade to say goodbye to the *QE2*. Apparently this was the first port she visited forty years earlier and the authorities wanted to give her a rousing send-off. The Captain was presented with a commemorative plaque, and he and many of the crew were driven in the cars on parade. As we sailed away, the ship gave her farewell blasts and all the cars sounded their horns in reply.

Sunday at sea meant that we went to the theatre for interdenominational church service. Unlike the growing trend for change on other ships, it was very traditional with proper hymn tunes and correct words. The cruise director read one lesson and the Captain another, both from the King James Bible.

Near to our table were some Japanese passengers. Opposite was a sweet couple who smiled and bowed their heads on greeting. The woman tried to speak English to the waiters, although they had menus printed in Japanese. Down below was a table of four and another couple close by. One man seemed to be in charge; maybe he was a travel rep, as he often came in with his briefcase as if he had been visiting his flock in another dining room. He had a very self-important manner and ordered the waiters and maître d' around in a piercing voice. Sometimes he disputed a dish and insisted on having the English version to check his own. The couple on the separate table were constantly being told by him what to order. We were amused to note that these two took to coming in early so that they could choose their own meal in peace. Bossyboots looked piqued when he arrived and found they were already eating.

Lisbon, which we had visited several times over the years, came and went with another ecstatic farewell. Towards the end of the voyage I decided to follow the Cunard Heritage Trail. The guide, Tomas, who looked like a posh version of stout Cortez, spoke excellent English but with a slight Spanish accent. Apparently this was the third Heritage Tour. Over 400 people had turned up for the first one, so a second group had to be arranged. Even so, there was a demand for a third tour.

Tomas spoke for over half an hour on the history of Cunard, going back to 1840 when Samuel Cunard won a contract to carry mail and passengers from Liverpool to New York. The first ships had a cow on board to supply fresh milk, chickens for eggs and a cat to catch the rats and stop them from eating the mail. From the earliest days the crew were given ginger to prevent seasickness.

We set off on the tour, which lasted an hour. We saw paintings, bronzes (including a head of the Queen by Oscar Nemon) and cabinets full of Cunard memorabilia, including one full of photographs of famous passengers, including royalty. There was a set of antique Japanese armour in gold and silver, which had been presented to the ship in 1979. Tapestries hung on walls, also many posters advertising Cunard ships down the years. In the midships lobby there was a silver model of the *QE2* made by Asprey's.

Tomas, who had an impressive voice as well as a figure, emphasised the treasures with expressive gestures. Every so often he would ask, "And where are they going in November? Are they going to a Cunard museum? No! Are they going back to the donors? No! To the City of Southampton? No! No! They are going with the ship to Dubai! Bah! Come! Come! We trotted after him to see yet more treasures, sad that they could not have been saved.

Before disembarking we said goodbye to our two excellent waiters, both leaving the ship to go home. We thanked the maître d' for his kindness. All were worried because they would be out of their jobs in November. Some might find posts on other ships, but the *Queen Mary* and the *Queen Victoria* were fully staffed and the next *Queen Elizabeth* was still in the planning stage.

The disembarkation was very orderly, and passengers waited in public rooms until they were called. There was something about the ship, unlike some others we have been on, which made people behave in a civilised fashion.

This was an enjoyable and relaxing cruise. Our only regret was that we did not sail on the *QE2* years before. It was a matter of *hail and farewell*.

CHAPTER NINE

THE GRAND TOUR

On our way down to Southampton I kept thinking of all the reasons why we did not like the *Aurora* the last time we sailed in her.

I decided to keep quiet lest Himself asked, "Whose bright idea was it to come on this cruise?"

After over twenty-five years of retirement in our dearly loved cottage, we had recently 'downsized' – a horrible word – and were finding it difficult to settle in the confines of an apartment. We decided to use some of the proceeds from the house sale on another long sea voyage. We were late in booking and, with no reasonable cabins left, we settled for a suite on the *Aurora*.

It was not until we were on board and being served with champagne and sandwiches that we realised this experience might be different from other cruises. A man arrived and introduced himself as Sanjay, our butler. He looked like an Indian version of Jeeves, as portrayed years ago by Stephen Fry. He was suave, with receding hair and a supercilious manner. There was no doubt that he gathered from the start that we were not used to butler services. Himself took an instant dislike to him and for the next three months left most of the communicating to me. After depositing our cases on the floor he enquired if Sir or Madam needed help with the unpacking and, receiving a negative answer, he shimmered off.

We examined the suite, which was more than twice the size of an ordinary cabin, with a large dining and sitting area, and a separate bedroom with full-length curtains to draw if required. In the bathroom was a Jacuzzi, a shower, a washbasin and, in an adjoining area, a loo and another washbasin.

There were three telephones (one situated at the side of the loo) and two televisions (one in the bedroom). As well as tourist literature, books, binoculars, and tea- and coffee-making equipment, there was a cache of writing paper embossed with our names and suite number. Outside was a double-length balcony with loungers, chairs and tables. To clean the whole area we had a jolly, smiling Indian steward called Michael.

After boat drill, Sanjay materialised with canapés, doubtless to be consumed before dinner along with the chocolates and champagne already in situ. We told him that we would not need canapés in future, and from the look on his face I understood that this was not the correct response. Later, he appeared with the menus for the next day and enquired if Sir or Madam would like breakfast served in the suite. Sir would not, but Madam would definitely like it.

The next morning he came in at the stated time and set out yogurt, cereal, fruit juice and croissants on the large dining table. Having ascertained my wishes, he poured out the coffee, sugared and stirred it, and then said, "Would Madam care to come for her breakfast?"

I thanked him and, as I sat down, I wondered how it was that I had never managed, in sixty years, to train Himself to present breakfast in such a way, or indeed to present breakfast at all.

In spite of being in a suite, our table for two in the dining room was only reserved for dinner. This meant queuing up before other meals and dashing in an unseemly manner to get the table of choice. Early in the voyage Himself came back after breakfast and reported he had been 'duffcd up', as he termed it, by a white-haired old lady who physically shoved him aside to get into the dining room first. At lunchtime she tried the same trick, but he stretched out his arm and held her back while he ushered in a young man in a wheelchair.

For the first time on any ship in which we had sailed there was a norovirus outbreak. The Captain announced that measures were being taken to combat it, and numerous passengers were confined to their cabins. The Captain's Cocktail Parties were cancelled, but that did not trouble us as we had not attended any for years.

I went to a lecture about Port Said and Cairo. The tours were listed on a screen and the speaker read from an autocue. The slides were dull and, as he talked about one tour after another, people got up and walked out after they had heard about their own choice. A women next to me fell asleep. I did not bother to waken her as she was not missing a great deal. Later I went to a lecture on Salalah and came away confused as to whether I had booked the correct tour. I had to go to the Tours Office to check. It was the correct one, but the speaker was so hell-bent on promoting each tour that he failed to deliver an overall picture. Oh, for the good old days when John McCarthy packed the cinemas and theatres with his riveting talks and slides!

At Barcelona, which we had visited several times, I did not go ashore. Sanjay was beginning to unbend and asked each morning how Madam was today. His duties with us were light, consisting of changing the flowers and bringing fresh fruit and the menus for the next day, and the Priority Disembarkation Cards in case we needed them. Perhaps he was kept busy 'butlering' in other suites.

After leaving Athens we had 'Pirate Drill', but the official description was 'Extra Drill to ensure the continuing safety of Passengers'. We had to close and lock the balcony doors and draw the curtains and stand or take a chair into the corridor until the checks were done. I had an interesting conversation with an elderly gentleman next door. He suggested that there must be plenty of Second World War veterans on board who could repel an attack. He said he was willing to volunteer, but would need a telescopic rifle as he had been a sniper. I replied that I doubted whether a cruise ship would have many of these in stock.

At Port Said we opened the curtains to find we were moored opposite an enormous block of flats. The roofs were covered with hundreds of television satellite dishes. I wandered ashore after the coaches had left for Cairo and thought the town was dirty, smelly and ugly. There were numerous stalls full of tourist tat, but my lasting memory is of all the poor, thin cats and kittens I saw. One forgets how neglected animals are in many countries.

The transit through the Suez Canal was interesting, but not as exciting as that through the Panama Canal. We reached the Great Bitter Lake, where we waited several hours for the northbound ships to pass. From the guide sheet we discovered that, when Ferdinand de Lesseps built the canal, Disraeli borrowed money from the Rothschilds and bought shares making Britain the largest individual shareholder. Of course this ended with the Suez crisis in 1956.

It was very hot and I opened the balcony doors to get a little air. As I stood there Sanjay appeared as if from nowhere and said reproachfully, "Madam will find that if she leaves the balcony doors open it will interfere with the air conditioning."

Madam thought, 'Blow the air conditioning!' but obediently closed the doors.

Gradually he unbent as the voyage continued and I learned that his wife was expecting a baby. I asked about it from time to time, and he assured me, "When I have any news, Madam will be the first to know."

During the hours of darkness all balcony curtains had to be drawn and the lights in the cabins dimmed. No doubt a brilliantly lit cruise ship would be seen by pirates miles away. All ships were shadowed through the Gulf of Aden by vessels of various nationalities. Our 'escort' included a Russian warship.

Sharm el Sheikh came and went. Oman was a country of contrasts, both in scenery and in architecture, but it was not geared up for tourists, which was a blessing. Herds of camels galloped about as we travelled the roads, and dozens of goats trotted in groups.

By the time we reached Muscat I was having to use a stick, owing to back problems and sciatica, and did not feel up to the long walk into the town. However, I managed a tour of Dubai and the words 'opulent' and 'amazing' sprang to mind. There were many tall, elegant skyscrapers and other beautiful buildings. It looked a prosperous place, but some unfinished projects had been mothballed. Sad it was to see the *QE2* moored ahead of the *Aurora*. She looked lonely and neglected. The money had run out, so the grandiose plans to turn her into a floating hotel were on hold.

When we reached Mumbai (formerly Bombay) Indian officials checked our credentials face-to-face. Before leaving the United Kingdom we had to fill in endless forms, pay an exorbitant fee, and send our passports and two extra photos to get a visa. Now every passenger, whether going ashore or not, had to fill in more forms and present them with cruise cards and passports to be stamped and approved.

It was Republic Day, marking sixty years since India became independent, when we landed. On the coach we passed quickly through some awful slum areas (a shanty town) and then saw some lovely old buildings including the railway station, the mint, the town hall and the Customs House, which dated back to 1720. The guide pointed these out with pride and everyone refrained from saying that they were built at the time of the British Raj. There were some beautiful modern buildings too and we passed the Taj Mahal Hotel, which had been attacked by terrorists the previous year.

On my return I rang for room service to ask for tea and biscuits. Twenty minutes later Sanjay appeared with them, looking perturbed and saying, "Madam should have telephoned me for this order. Madam has my private telephone number on the desk."

I expect room service had recognised the suite number and told him to deal with it. I felt that I should never master the etiquette of this 'butlering' business.

At Port Kelang hundreds of passengers got off the ship to go on tours to Kuala Lumpur. Later, more took the shuttle bus to the shopping mall in town. I decided to conserve my energy for Singapore, having visited KL years earlier.

The arrangements for getting off the ship at various ports were chaotic. On other vessels passengers waited in allotted areas (the theatre or cinema) until their tour was called. Then they were led off in an orderly manner. Here the atrium was heaving with people, some wanting to get ashore to fly home, some going on tours and some clamouring to get off to catch a shuttle bus. It was pandemonium and complaints to the reception desk and Tours Office did not alter the situation for several weeks.

At Singapore I went on a Battlefields Tour. The guide was informative, though her narrative was harrowing at times. I had always understood that Singapore fell because the guns were pointing out to sea and the Japanese came down from the north through Malaysia. The reasons were more complex and included the fact that their well-trained troops were more used to jungle warfare, the British lacked equipment and didn't prepare adequately, the new naval base was without ships, and the generals were incompetent. Apparently the lights of Singapore were not blacked out in case it affected morale; hence the city was lit up like a Christmas tree when the first bombs fell in December 1941.

At Kranji Reservoir Park there was a huge war memorial and the numerous graves are beautifully kept by the War Graves Commission. Photos, drawings and letters tell the horrific story of those incarcerated in Changi Jail. There was a replica of the simple Changi Chapel, where people left small posies and crosses. I thought of our friends Reg and Don, who had been captured and held in the jail before being sent to work on the infamous Burma Railway. Reg was in a POW camp near Hiroshima when the atom bomb was dropped. Don was so emaciated at the end of the war he was kept in hospital for three months until he was flown home.

We arrived back at the ship emotionally and physically exhausted. I rang to ask Sanjay to bring me some tea and cakes. He rang back to say that cakes were unavailable, but he would bring some fruit instead. "So much better for Madam than cakes."

As I was becoming less mobile and had to use a stick to get around, at Vietnam I cancelled the tour to Ho Chi Minh city. We docked at Phu My, having sailed up the Mekong river. Opposite our balcony was an endless vista of jungle. I caught a bus to the small town of Vung Tau, about a thirty-minute drive away. In between stretches of swamp and scrubland were shanty towns, garages, workshops and other small businesses. Nearer the town were some beautiful houses and churches and a Chinese temple.

The traffic was very heavy, but among it I saw one man leading a bullock. Another had a triangular skip on the front of his bicycle. It was full of wood and he could just see over the top. Looking at the tree-clad mountains, the jungle and the swamps, it seemed quite beautiful, but it was very hot and humid. I made a few purchases at some stalls. It was ironic that the only foreign currency the traders would accept was American dollars.

After a day at sea we anchored in Halong Bay, reckoned to be the eighth wonder of the world. Somehow the town was reminiscent of French coastal places like Cannes. On closer inspection some of the modern buildings looked ramshackle, but there were some lovely old houses.

After the war, while he was still in the Royal Marine

Commando, Himself had been stationed in Hong Kong. He had been prepared for change, but not for the skyscrapers and the busy port with the ferries plying to and fro.

As usual I went alone on the tour, which took us to the Peak Tram, supposed to be the steepest funicular railway in the world. At the top of Victoria Heights we could see the whole of Hong Kong and Hong Kong Island. After a spectacular drive down, we spent time in Stanley Market and went on to Aberdeen to see the junks and sampans; we had a short sail on one.

The next day my back and legs were so painful I had to go to the medical centre. Painkillers and instructions to 'rest, rest, rest' were suggested. Himself persuaded me not to go ashore again in Hong Kong. After serious thought I decided to cancel one of the highlights of the cruise – a visit to the Great Wall of China. Usually the tours staff are anxious to sell their tickets, but this time a young man was anxious to point out the disadvantages: a very early start, a long coach drive, cold weather, perhaps nowhere to sit. All these might give me problems, he suggested.

I said, "In other words you mean that the Chinese would not be too happy about having to stretcher an old lady off the Wall?"

He grinned and said, "That's about it."

I got a full refund.

We tied up at Xingang at 5.30 a.m. and the tours left soon after. It was bitterly cold and on the port side the water was covered with thick blocks of ice. In the evening, when we sailed out of harbour, a series of thuds and bumps was caused by ice floes banging against the ship.

The bureaucracy of the Japanese emigration was time-consuming and frustrating. They checked paperwork, fingerprinting and biometric data for everyone, whether going ashore or not. At Hiroshima there was another bureaucratic hold-up when officials decided that everyone must have a temperature check before anyone left the ship.

Hiroshima had risen phoenix-like from atomic rubble to become a prosperous modern city. We visited the Peace Memorial Park, the Peace Dome and the Peace Museum. Visitors walked through the museum in silence while reviewing the gruesome results of 6 August 1945, when almost everything was flattened in seconds. All those at the epicentre of the blast were incinerated and 150,000 more victims died within a few months in dreadful agony. It was horrendous to learn even some of the details. Hiroshima was on a par with our visit to Pearl Harbor some years earlier – thought-provoking and horrifying at the same time.

Osaka and Okinawa involved more Japanese red tape and more encounters between officials and furious passengers. Meanwhile, I was having deep muscular massages, a herbal foot soak, hot-stone therapy and acupuncture to try to ease the pain in my back and legs. Himself borrowed a wheelchair and then we moved around on board with some alacrity. The problem was that it (and I) could not go ashore owing to lack of insurance of the vehicles.

One morning Sanjay bounced in to announce that his wife had given birth to a son. We offered him our sincere best wishes.

At each port of call in Australia and Tasmania I had fond memories of our last visits, although this time I was not able to go ashore. Sydney brought back memories of *Orpheus in the Underworld* at the opera house. Melbourne reminded us of George, whom we met years earlier on a world cruise. We kept in touch for a long time, but I feared he had gone to the great cruise ship in the sky as I had had no replies to recent letters, e-mails or phone calls.

At Adelaide, Himself got off the ship and took the shuttle bus into town with instructions to get postcards and any items of interest. It was one of life's little experiences for him. After a forty-minute ride and a long walk to the market stalls he returned empty-handed with the message, "Only tourist rubbish and T-shirts at £20 each."

Each morning Sanjay brought my breakfast. He had unbent quite a bit and smiled from time to time. The Australian yogurts were very creamy and delicious and I commented upon them.

A couple of mornings later he said, "As the yogurts are so popular, Madam, the restaurants have nearly run out of them. Therefore I have taken the liberty of depositing some in your fridge."

Well done, Jeeves!

After Australia we headed back to Singapore and more 'Pirate Drill' before making a mad dash through the Strait of Malacca in darkness. On the promenade deck there were hosepipes leading up to the lifeboats, and at each end of the ship were large cupboards containing noise repellents. We were told they were ten times louder than a jumbo jet.

It was very hot as we crossed the Indian Ocean and not a ship was seen for days. Male, the capital of the Maldives, was not much of a place, according to returning passengers. It was a strict Islamic country and warnings were issued to ladies about covering up and exposing as little flesh as possible.

When the weather was good, Himself used to wheel me out on to the promenade deck, where we spent time relaxing and reading. Mauritius and Madagascar passed without our noticing the ninety-five-degree temperatures as we sat in the shade. I was eating less and less as the extravagant language of the menus bore little relation to the food on the plates. Himself sent back the meat five times as it could not be cut, even with steak knives. Many passengers grumbled. The soups were of three colours – green, brown and khaki – and with anything in pastry only the filling was edible; the pastry itself could not be broken by spoon or fork. We had never experienced such poor food on a ship in all our years at sea.

At Durban a group in full Zulu rig chanted and did war dances on the quayside for three hours. What a racket it was! A cold wind was blowing at Cape Town and eventually the weather worsened and the pilots refused to take the ship out of the harbour. We left there fifteen hours later than scheduled, and had to take an extra day to get to Walvis Bay, Namibia. I recalled the lovely pink flamingoes and the sand dunes from our last visit. Walvis Bay is the only sheltered deep harbour along that part of the African coastline, which is termed the Skeleton Coast because it is littered with many shipwrecks.

As we neared the end of the voyage, Himself contacted the purser and arranged for a wheelchair and help to convey me ashore. At Madeira it poured with rain and the wind reached thirty-four knots. As ever, the last day dragged once the cases were packed. Sanjay came in and graciously received his envelope containing his tip. At dinner we gave our hard-working waiters their rewards and handed an envelope to Michael, our smiling steward. He told me he would be praying for my return to good health and gave me a jar of foul-smelling gunge to rub on my back and legs.

We arrived back in Southampton and left the ship with Priority Disembarkation Cards. Both of us were wondering if this would be our final voyage. *Time would tell.*

SUNSET

Himself and I are still cruising, in spite of the fact that I am disabled. We opt for shorter voyages instead of the long, lazy weeks of former years. In the last eighteen months we have been round the British Isles, into the Mediterranean and down to the Canary Islands for Christmas, ending up in Madeira for the fantastic New Year's Eve firework display. With two sticks or a small 'walker' I manage to get about on most ships. Both on board and on shore I have been amazed at the kindness of strangers. People offer to help even when I can cope on my own. Going ashore is more of a problem and the day-long tours are not really feasible. Last year, wandering around on Kirkwall in the Orkneys, I hit a paving stone with my 'walker'. It flew in one direction and I flew in another, both landing with a thud. Three youths rushed to pick me up and escorted me to a seat. One checked the 'walker' and another offered to get a brandy from a nearby pub. They had rings in their noses and ears and sported weird haircuts, but could not have been more caring.

Himself and I have been fortunate to be able to travel for so long and to see so much of the world. We have made many, many good friends – some no longer with us, others who keep in touch. We are grateful for the happy memories we share with them. We realise that our cruising days are coming to an end, though we have booked a couple of voyages for the months ahead. Maybe we shall make them, maybe not.

As the old lady I met in Reid's Palace said, "At my age one must have something to which one can look forward."

As we move forward towards the sunset I agree with her wholeheartedly.